Anna looked so sincere

So willing to fight for him to believe in them, just as she always seemed so willing to fight for Colm.

Liam suddenly wanted to lean over the coffee table to close the distance between them...and kiss her. The urge caught him totally unaware. It wasn't that he hadn't noticed that Anna was attractive. That smile and laugh—he couldn't shake them. A guy would have to be dead not to appreciate either feature. And he'd quickly begun to admire that she was good at her job—good with his brother.

But wanting to kiss her?

No. The temptation was a surprise, but not one he could indulge in. Instead, he reached out and simply placed his hand on top of hers.

Maybe...

Dear Reader,

My family once had a very special neighbor, Tiffany. My kids and their friends accepted her without question. She didn't verbalize much, but she always had a smile and an utter fascination with watches. One day my kids and their friends came running to the house to get me because a group of strangers were picking on Tiff. We went out and with a few mom-threats on my part, they left. In that moment, the kids showed not just compassion, but they showed that they knew that different isn't something to be afraid of or mocked...it's special. I was so very proud of all of them!

Here we're introduced to the Sunrise Foundation, whose goal is to help exceptional people lead exceptional lives. Instead of locating the story in Erie, I used the fictional neighboring town of Whedon—the setting of last November's *Unexpected Gifts,* because Erie already has an organization that helps our special residents—the Gertrude A. Barber National Institute. They do such wonderful work. And in neighboring Buffalo, New York, there's SASi. Suburban Adult Service, Inc. Harlequin's Distribution Center has a number of SASi clients working there and when I visited the Buffalo warehouse, it was a true pleasure to meet some of them.

In this story, Anna and Liam both believe that they know what's best for Liam's brother, Colm. In the end it's Colm who teaches them an important life lesson—that you need to stand up for what you want and love with all your heart!

Holly Jacobs

A One-of-a-Kind Family
Holly Jacobs

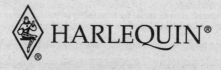

HARLEQUIN®

TORONTO • NEW YORK • LONDON
AMSTERDAM • PARIS • SYDNEY • HAMBURG
STOCKHOLM • ATHENS • TOKYO • MILAN • MADRID
PRAGUE • WARSAW • BUDAPEST • AUCKLAND

Recycling programs
for this product may
not exist in your area.

ISBN-13: 978-0-373-78360-1

A ONE-OF-A-KIND FAMILY

Copyright © 2010 by Holly Fuhrmann.

www.eHarlequin.com

Printed in U.S.A.

ABOUT THE AUTHOR

In 2000, Holly Jacobs sold her first book to Harlequin Enterprises. She's since sold more than twenty-five novels to the publisher. Her romances have won numerous awards and made the Waldenbooks bestseller list. In 2005, Holly won a prestigious Career Achievement Award from *RT Book Reviews*. In her nonwriting life Holly is married to a police captain, and together they have four children. Visit Holly at www.HollyJacobs.com, or you can snail-mail her at P.O. Box 11102, Erie, PA 16514-1102.

Books by Holly Jacobs

HARLEQUIN SUPERROMANCE
1511—SAME TIME NEXT SUMMER
1601—UNEXPECTED GIFTS

HARLEQUIN AMERICAN ROMANCE
1232—ONCE UPON A THANKSGIVING
1238—ONCE UPON A CHRISTMAS
1247—ONCE UPON A VALENTINE'S

HARLEQUIN EVERLASTING
THE HOUSE ON BRIAR HILL ROAD

CHAPTER ONE

"WE GOT the house," Anna Chapel practically sang as she burst into The Sunrise Foundation's small reception area. The first thing that caught her eye was the big sign that boldly and proudly announced: Sunrise Foundation, Helping Exceptional People Lead Exceptional Lives.

Today's news was certainly going to go a long way toward helping a small group of Whedon, Pennsylvania's exceptional people lead more independent, and certainly exceptional, lives.

"It's ours," she sang out again. "We got it."

Anna was so excited she couldn't contain the feeling any longer and wiggled her hips. There were some things in life that Anna felt she was blessed with, but there were others she knew she was not. Rhythm and her hair were two of the "were-not" areas. She wiggled her hips again and felt a few more of her Medusa curls escape her ponytail, but she was simply too happy to mind.

"Was that a dance?" her friend Deanne Cellino, Ceelie as she was known, laughed. "Because if it was…" She shook her head and her long blond hair swished back and forth along her shoulders—shoulders that were so much higher than Anna's five-foot-five-inch frame. Anna always thought of Ceelie as a bit Amazonian—she looked like a warrior, but had the heart of an earth mother. She always got warm and fuzzy over the small things.

"Hey, that was a Snoopy Dance of Joy, my friend. And you're not going to dim my absolute glee by pointing out that I have no sense of rhythm. If there was such a thing as an anti-rhythm, I realize that's what I'd have. But when one is dancing a Snoopy Dance, all you need is joy and I've got that. Come on."

She grabbed Ceelie's hands and Snoopy-danced again. Ceelie was laughing so hard that all she did was stand there, but she finally got herself under control and did a bit of a jig as well.

"You are absolutely crazy, girl," Ceelie assured Anna with a friend's affection.

"I might be, but you're talking to a crazy person who got the house. It's so perfect, Ceelie. Three bedrooms, two full baths. A ranch, so with the addition of a ramp, it's handicap-accessible and it's—"

"Perfect," Ceelie filled in for her.

Anna sighed, still riding the glow of her success. "Yes, perfect for our clients. It will make a great group home."

All her joyful dancing had drained off enough of her excess energy that Anna could sit down. She plopped onto the small loveseat in the reception area. "Now, the work begins. We need to get our variance from the zoning board, then start the renovations and…" Her sentence faded as she started mulling over the long list of jobs that lay ahead of her.

"Listen, enjoy the moment. Don't worry too much about what's coming up and what's behind you. Live in the now."

"Deanne Cellino, ladies and gentlemen," Anna said to a nonexistent audience, "mystic, sage, warrior princess and all-around advisor to the world."

Ceelie blew a raspberry in her direction. "You know I'm right."

"Yes, I do." Anna studied her friend. Ceelie liked to say she was vertically challenged, but her abundance of height was needed to contain her giant spirit. Ceelie was one of those people who always seemed to have things together. She balanced a demanding job and parenting two children with apparent ease.

Anna and Ceelie made up the entire staff of The Sunrise Foundation. Anna and Ceelie served as life coaches. Ceelie had come up with the job title and Anna always thought it was an apt description for a job that varied based on each client's highly individual medical and emotional needs.

Ceelie's smile faded a bit. "And not that I'm anxious to bring down your happy mood, but your mother called."

"Oh." Anna forced a smile she didn't feel. Her mother calling during a work day never boded well. "Did she say what she wants?"

"She wants you to call her back as soon as possible. She said she tried your cell, but it went to voice mail."

"I turned it off at my meeting with the real-

estate agent, haven't turned it back on yet."
She reached in her bag, pulled out the phone
and switched it on, then scrolled through the
missed calls—four from her mother. No, this
did not bode well.

"You should probably give her a call. You
have an appointment in half an hour with
that new case." Ceelie somehow honed in on
the correct file that was midway through a
huge stack and handed it to her. "A thirty-
year-old who's been in his brother's custody
for two years since their parents died in a
car accident."

Anna looked at the file labeled Colm
Franklin. She opened it and found that other
than an initial fact sheet, it was empty.
Normally clients came to Sunrise with all
kinds of documentation from other programs.
"No notes?"

"None. He was in special-ed classes back
in high school. Long before Whedon practiced mainstreaming. Once he finished
school, he stayed home with his mother."

"Oh. Do we have anything from the school?"

"It's so long ago at this point that it's not
really worth much—that would be my

thought. Though you can call and see what the school has."

"Even if I find something, I'm basically starting from scratch, right?" She shut the folder.

"Yes, that's about the gist of it."

"Any insights on the brother?" Family members called Sunrise for a variety of reasons. It helped to know what they wanted from the program.

The Sunrise Foundation was a small non-profit organization that survived on a shoe-string budget with grants from both government and charitable foundations. The money for the new group home came from a huge grant last year. Ceelie had become a grant-writing pro, but there was never quite enough money to accomplish everything they'd like to do. And at Sunrise, everything was pretty much anything. From helping clients find housing, to teaching them to handle money, to helping some learn basic life-skills. Anna had taught clients to cook, to use a cell phone and even to tie their shoes. They'd helped place clients in jobs, and… Basically they facilitated whatever a particular client needed to improve their quality of life.

Anna's job description changed on a daily basis for each of her fifteen clients. And the amount of time she worked with each client changed as well. Some needed more intense interaction, some just minimal support.

"Liam Franklin, the brother, is self-employed. Something to do with computers and security." Ceelie shrugged. "You know me and technology."

Anna did know. Ceelie could manage a word processor or spreadsheet on the computer, but other than that, she did nothing more complex than e-mail.

"Liam works out of his home office most of the time, but he has to travel for business and is looking for a babysitter for Colm when he does. He got a referral from his doctor, and assured me in no uncertain terms that he wanted nothing more than that. Just a baby-sitter."

Anna ran her fingers through her wildly springy hair. For years she'd tried products, haircuts, flat irons…. Finally, she'd reached the ripe old age of twenty-eight and admitted that she didn't have the time. She was going to embrace her outer Medusa and let her hair live the life it was destined to lead. After all, that was her job too: helping people lead the best lives they were capable of. She looked at the Sunrise motto again. Helping Exceptional People Lead Exceptional Lives.

It was such a simple concept, and so succinct. Too bad some families never understood it.

She wondered what kind of person Colm's brother—who simply wanted a babysitter—was. Maybe this new client was so severely limited that he needed that kind of care, but maybe he could do more… That sense of the possible, the idea of helping someone discover they could accomplish more than they ever imagined—that's what kept Anna doing what she did.

"Just a babysitter," she murmured, more to herself than to Ceelie.

"You can handle it," Ceelie, a Pollyanna in disguise, said.

Anna nodded. "Sure. I'll do what's best for…" She glanced at the file. "Colm. Colm Franklin. After I call my mother back."

"Colm doesn't know how lucky he is," Ceelie assured her.

Anna hoped *lucky* was the word Colm and his brother would someday use to describe their first meeting at Sunrise.

She got up and headed for her private office to call her mother. Although, she was already sure that there was some new crisis— one that probably involved a man in one way or another. She couldn't remember who her mother's current boyfriend was. The names changed so frequently, it was hard to keep up.

"Hey, Anna," Ceelie hollered.

Anna turned around and looked at her friend, who did another little Snoopy Dance. "You got the house."

Anna's spirit immediately lifted. "You're right, we got the house."

LIAM FRANKLIN pulled up in front of the small brick office front on Main Street. Whedon, Pennsylvania, was a small town south of Erie. There wasn't much to it, so he knew he must have driven by this building every day for years, yet he'd never noticed the sign in the window that proclaimed The

Sunrise Foundation, with a rainbow and sun framing the words.

He checked the business card again.

Colm had lived with Liam since their parents died. Because Liam ran his computer security firm from home, things had gone well until work demanded he travel more. Taking Colm with him wasn't an option, and his day-help, Aunt Betty, didn't like staying overnight. So, Liam had contacted Colm's physician, thinking he might know of a babysitter who'd had experience working with people with special needs. The doctor had referred him to The Sunrise Foundation, and he'd talked to some woman named Ceelie there who had set up this appointment with this life coach, Anna Chapel.

This Anna Chapel had been assigned his brother's case.

He didn't like that Colm was in the system. Well, not really in the system. Sunrise was a private foundation that came very highly recommended. The fact that it was a community-based organization meant it was able to provide resources that each individual needed. Well, Colm didn't need anything except someone to stay with him when Liam was out of town, an occurrence that was happening more frequently.

Balancing his job and his brother's needs made him really feel for working single parents. It seemed there was never a minute that he wasn't doing something…and often he was five steps behind.

Liam walked into the office and a bell above the front door rang merrily. He stood in the reception area. There was a loveseat and a desk with a phone and computer. But the walls…the walls were amazing. They were decorated with framed pictures ranging from childish scrawls to a few more practiced ones. He was studying a particularly pretty sunrise—or maybe sunset—over a large body of water, when someone cleared their throat behind him.

Liam turned and found a woman with the biggest hair he'd ever seen standing in a doorway, smiling at him. Her hair wasn't really styled big on purpose—you didn't need to be a hairdresser to see that. Rather it was big in a too-many-curls-for-one-small-head-to-have sort of way.

"Well, hello," the woman said. "Welcome to Sunrise. How can I help you?" The words tumbled over one another in a single breath. She exuded a boundless energy that she seemed to try hard to contain.

"I have a meeting with Anna Chapel."

"Oh, you must be Liam Franklin." She hurried to him, thrust a hand out and continued, "It's so nice to meet you. Let's go to my office and see what we can do for you and your brother, Colm."

He shook her hand, then followed her through the reception area, trying not to notice how her myriad of curls bounced about her head as she walked. If he were back in second grade, the urge to pull one and watch it spring back in place would have been too much to resist. But he was thirty and here on adult business.

Anna led him to a neat office. The desk and shelves were immaculately organized. So neat in fact that they almost looked sterile. But these walls were completely covered in artwork as well. The overall effect was anything but sterile. It was happy art. He couldn't help but notice a lot of sunrises and rainbows.

She followed his gaze and smiled. "We ask our clients to make us pictures. It helps the office feel like home, don't you think?"

Before he could answer, she added, "The picture out front that you were studying was made by Josh Hampton. He's a talented artist despite the limitations he has with his hands. Most of our clients are far more enthusiastic than gifted, but we treasure all our pictures."

She gestured toward a chair and then, rather than going behind her desk, she took the chair next to it. "I've got the papers you sent over, and everything looks like it's in order."

"Great. So you've got a babysitter for us, or can get one?" he asked, somewhat anxiously.

Her smile faded and she shook her head. "Yes. But while Sunrise will be able to help you find respite care, we offer so much more. I'd like to schedule a meeting with your brother as soon as possible. His file is very light. We could do a few tests and—"

The urge to spring to his feet and leave was almost overwhelming. Liam resisted. He clutched the arm of the chair and forced himself to speak softly and slowly. "Listen, Ms. Chapel, I didn't come to you in order to have my brother assessed in any way. He went through all that years ago. Well, Colm is special and he's not something you can label and chart. He's not an IQ number or any other sort of definition you want to assign him. He's a person. A totally unique person. So I don't want your tests. And I really don't want him to be some name on a file. All I need is someone able to deal with his particular needs when I have to travel. I was told that your foundation could see to that."

"We can help you with that," she assured him. "But we offer so much more. We can help your brother—"

"Colm. His name is Colm. Not 'the patient' or 'the client.' He's far more than either of those things."

"Mr. Franklin, the last thing I want to do is make you feel that your brother would be or is simply a client or file for me. My job is to help Colm be as self-sufficient as he can. Sunrise Foundation's purpose is what our mission statement says—we help exceptional people lead exceptional lives. We provide advice and assistance with every aspect of housing, employment, medical care, education—"

"Colm has me," Liam assured her. Even before his parents died, he'd always known Colm was ultimately his responsibility. And he was willing to do whatever he had to in order to keep his brother happy and content. "I'm all he needs. And all I need is some help—"

"I'm not trying to railroad you into anything. I simply want to meet your brother and see what, if anything, we can offer him in order to make his life better. And that's what you want, right? To see Colm live his life to its full potential?"

Okay, so what could he say to that? What he wanted to say was back off and leave them alone. They were doing fine.

What he wanted to do was tear up the papers he'd signed for Sunrise and take the manila folder that had Colm's name on the tab away from this curly-haired, smiling woman.

They were fine.

Granted, he'd never planned on assuming total responsibility for his brother so soon. He could still remember the day. His parents had gone to a show in Buffalo and he'd been staying with Colm. At some point, Liam had drifted off. He'd awakened disoriented when there was a knock on the door and he'd opened it to find a policeman with a sober expression standing on the porch.

"Mr. Franklin?" It took Liam a moment to realize that Ms. Chapel was saying his name, not the cop from the past.

He shut out the sad memory. "Fine. You can meet him, but tread lightly. I don't want him upset. Since we lost my parents two years ago, I've worked hard to see to it he's got a sense of stability and normalcy."

"Mr. Franklin, honestly, I'm a life coach. My only goal is to help your brother, not upset him." She stood and extended her hand. "I'll see you at your place tomorrow at nine, if that works for you."

He didn't want to shake her hand. It felt as if he'd be agreeing to let her into their lives, even after tomorrow. But she stood there, hand extended a fraction of a second longer than he'd probably have waited, and he found himself taking it anyway.

"I'm only agreeing to let you arrange for a babysitter, and to meet him tomorrow," he warned her. "It's only a meeting."

She nodded, her curly hair boinging every

which way. "Let's start with tomorrow and take it from there."

She escorted him to the front door and waved as he left. Just the motion of her hand was enough to set her shoulder-length curls bouncing.

Liam left the office not sure what had happened.

He'd simply wanted to arrange a babysitter.

And he was leaving with Anna Chapel coming to the house tomorrow.

No. That meeting hadn't gone the way he'd expected.

CHAPTER TWO

THE NEXT DAY, Anna arrived at the Franklin house promptly at nine. She was as prepared as she could possibly be. She'd read Colm's thin file. He'd been oxygen deprived at birth. The medical term was hypoxia, but medical definitions weren't her concern.

He'd been labeled slow by one doctor, intellectually disabled by another. The last assessment had placed his cognitive age at eight. She put all those previous reports aside. She didn't care how he'd been tested and labeled. She only cared about how she could use that knowledge to help Colm live his life to the fullest.

His brother, Liam, had certainly been on the defensive yesterday. Anna knew some people might find it off-putting, but she found the way he defended his brother attractive. Unfortunately, it was just one of many qualities she found attractive about Liam Franklin. But since he was Colm's guardian… No, she couldn't think of him as attractive in any way.

She took a long, deep breath to clear the image of Liam from her thoughts and instead, concentrated on the weather.

It was one of those balmy, mid-April days that made it easy to believe another winter was officially over.

The minute she saw the Franklins' white two-story house surrounded by a blaze of red tulips, she was struck by a case of porch envy.

Some people dreamed about picket fences or tons of acreage or living in the right fashionable neighborhood.

Anna dreamed about porches.

Porches like this one.

It extended at least eight feet away from the house, and wasn't simply a front porch, it was a wrap-around one as far as Anna could see from the sidewalk.

Of course, the porch was a bit barren-looking. Only two old folding lawn chairs sat on it, and the paint had long since started fading and peeling. But with a little elbow grease…

Someday.

Someday she'd move out of her apartment and buy her own house with a huge front porch. Then she'd paint it some merry color—maybe green—and furnish it with big white wicker furniture that had overstuffed cushions. In the mornings she'd sit on the porch, have a cup of coffee and read her paper before going into work. Then in the evenings, she'd come home, and after dinner, she'd be on her porch watching the day turn to dusk and maybe smiling at neighbors who strolled by.

Anna sighed. It was a lovely fantasy.

But right now, she didn't have time for fantasy. She had a job to do.

She walked onto the beautiful object of her porch envy and rang the doorbell. A matronly looking lady who reminded Anna faintly of Aunt Bee on the *Andy Griffith Show* answered the door. Tinier even than Anna, and roundish, the woman had salt-and-pepper hair, with a heavier emphasis on the salt. When she saw Anna, she smiled and a pair of dimples swallowed her cheeks. "Hello, you must be Ms. Chapel. Come in, dear."

Once Anna was inside, the woman introduced herself. "I'm Betty Taylor."

The fact that Anna had a mere second ago thought that the woman resembled Sheriff Andy Taylor's aunt on the Andy Griffith show made her smile.

"Liam wanted to be here, but he had a last-minute emergency with some local account and had to go. He wasn't very happy he couldn't be here to meet you himself."

Anna almost laughed at one of the biggest understatements she'd ever heard. She was positive that Liam had wanted to be here to monitor her meeting with Colm.

"He said you'd be coming and that you'd be wanting to meet our Colm," the woman continued. "This way, dear."

She showed Anna into the living room where there was a man who looked remarkably like Liam Franklin. More than remarkably like him—he looked exactly like Liam. They were twins. Somewhere around five-ten. Dark-brown hair and very blue eyes that were so much more open—happier—than Liam's had seemed. Where Liam peered at her distrustfully, this man smiled as he got up from his Lego and hurried over to her. "Hi, I'm Colm."

"And I'm Anna."

He hugged her and said, "Hi, Anna. You wanna play Legos?"

"Why don't I let you two talk," Mrs. Taylor said and left them alone.

"Aunt Betty is makin' cookies for us. She said we feed company. Aunt Betty likes to feed people. She really likes feedin' company, but we don't have much of that since Mommy and Daddy went to heaven. Liam, he's too busy for company."

As if that was all the introduction and information Anna needed, Liam returned to his building bricks. When she didn't immediately follow, he waved his hand in her direction impatiently. "Come on."

Anna sat down next to him on the floor and surveyed the pile of blocks. "So what are we playing?"

"I'm building a magic school like they got on the Wizards show I like. It's on Disney, and Liam likes Disney 'cause there ain't no bad words, so I get to watch it lots. I need the blue bricks."

For the next hour Anna sat on the floor digging through a huge pile of Lego for the blue bricks, and handing them to Colm as she asked him questions about his likes and dislikes, how he filled his days.

She wasn't sure what Liam had expected, but she always assessed her clients in as gentle a manner as possible. At thirty, Colm had long since passed the school system and his family had never enrolled him in any other community program or activities. "…and then I eat lunch. Sometimes, Liam's here and works, but sometimes he works someplace not here and it's me and Aunt Betty." He dropped his voice to a very loud stage whisper and said, "She's not really my aunt, but I love her, so she sorta is, and it's okay to call her aunt, Liam says. Liam says our family is sorta small, so addin' an aunt is good."

"Liam says." It was the phrase that had punctuated their hour-long conversation.

"Liam says bedtime's at nine."

"Liam says vegetables before dessert."

"Liam says don't answer the door."

Liam said a lot of things. And the things he said seemed to illustrate a deep sense of caring and commitment for his brother. As bristly as he'd been with Anna, she suspected that he had an entirely different demeanor here with Colm.

It was easy to see that he strived to give Colm a stable, loving home. But Anna suspected Colm could do more than what his brother thought.

"Aunt Betty came to help after Mommy and Daddy went to the angels." For a moment, Colm stopped building and looked at her with the first trace of sadness she'd seen in him. "I miss 'em."

"My father is with the angels, too," Anna told him. She'd only been sixteen when her father passed away. "I miss him, but it's nice to think he's watching over me."

"Yeah, Liam says Mommy was always watchin' me, so why would her being with angels stop her? He says that she's probably makin' the angels come watch me, too. She really loved me."

Anna chased away the memories of losing her father. She'd long since come to terms with it, and though she missed him, she remembered the good times more than the pain. "I bet she did, Colm."

"Liam says you're gonna help find me a babysitter for when Aunt Betty can't come. She don't like spendin' too many nights away from Mr. Taylor, 'cause he gets lonely."

"Is that what you want, Colm?" Anna asked. "Someone to come stay with you?"

Colm seemed confused by her question. "That's what Liam says. A babysitter for me is what we need."

"Yes, it is. But what do you *want?*"

Colm stood up and started to leave the room. "I wanna get some of those cookies and milk. You want some?"

"Sure."

He took her into the kitchen and said, "Aunt Betty, we want some cookies and milk, please."

"You two have a seat and I'll get them—"

Anna needed to get a feel for what Colm could do, so she said, "Actually, Mrs. Taylor. I was hoping you'd come sit with me for a minute. Maybe Colm would get us both some cookies and milk?"

Colm frowned. "I don't pour milk, 'cause I make a mess."

"Tell you what, you pour the milk and if

you make a mess, I'll help you clean it up," Anna promised.

Colm looked to Mrs. Taylor. She nodded and motioned Anna to join her at the table.

Both women watched Colm go to the cabinet and take one glass out, walk it to the island, then go back for another….

"Mrs. Taylor, I'm sure Mr. Franklin told you why I was here."

Her eyes never leaving Colm, Mrs. Taylor said, "Yes. I love Colm with all my heart, but I can't be with him as much as Liam needs me to be. Daytimes are fine, since Mr. Taylor has his club, but he likes me home at night, and to be honest, I'm old enough that I need to be home at night. I like going to sleep in my own bed, in my own house."

"I understand, Mrs. Taylor. I need to ask you honestly, do you think Colm is living up to his full potential?"

"Until this very moment, I wouldn't have even asked myself that."

Colm had all three glasses lined up in perfect order on the counter. He got out the half-gallon container of milk, left the refrig-

erator door open and slowly removed the cap from the carton.

"Colm, you should probably shut the door to the fridge," Anna said, then looked back to Mrs. Taylor who was still watching Colm pour the first glass of milk perfectly.

"Maybe we have coddled him. He's doing fine, isn't he?"

When all three glasses were poured, Colm put the lid back on the plastic container, returned it to the refrigerator and carried the glasses over one at a time.

He started to pick up cookies from the rack that they were cooling on, and Anna said, "It's probably more polite to put them on a plate, Colm."

"Oh, yeah. Aunt Betty always does that." He hurried off to the cupboard and grabbed a salad plate, piled it high with a stack of cookies, and with one hand on the top of the pile, and the other holding the plate, made his way to the table. He set the plate down carefully, but when he took his hand off the stack, the cookies tumbled. "Oh, no, I goofed. I can't—"

Anna picked up a cookie and put it back on

the plate. "Hey, cookies fall. No biggie. If they fall, you pick them up."

"Ten-second rule?" he asked Mrs. Taylor.

"They're not on the floor but the table, so there's a lot more than ten seconds when something falls on a table," the older woman assured him.

Colm broke into a smile and repiled the cookies. He looked proud as he announced, "There, I did it."

"You did," Anna agreed.

"I didn't even spill the milk. I was real careful."

"You did great," she told him. "But even if you'd made a mess, you could have cleaned it up. If you spill milk, you wipe it up."

"Yeah. If you knock cookies down you pick them up, and if you make a mess, you clean it."

Anna hadn't realized he was going to take her off-the-cuff comments to heart. She'd have to remember that. "Right, Colm. Everyone has accidents. All that matters is that when you do, you clean them up and try to do better the next time."

They all ate their cookies, and Anna caught Mrs. Taylor giving her furtive looks as if she were trying to decide whether Anna would be good for Colm. Anna suspected if Mrs. Taylor decided that she wouldn't be good for him, she'd be as fierce defending Colm as Liam had been.

When they finished, Colm said, "Hey, I'll clean up 'cause I brought it all over. I can do it."

"I'm sure you can, Colm," Anna told him. "Thank you."

He looked to Mrs. Taylor and the older woman offered him another dimple-filled smile. "That's lovely, Colm. I'm going to sit here and let you wait on me."

"Yeah, I'll do that 'cause you're old and get tired. Aunt Betty's feet ache sometimes and she moans like this," he made a loud wailing sound, and continued, "so maybe if I help, her old feet'll feel better, huh?"

"I'm sure they will, Colm." Anna tried desperately not to grin.

Mrs. Taylor watched as Colm tidied up. "It never occurred to me to let him help. His mother, Maire, was a dear friend, and she waited on him hand and foot, and when I started to help Liam out after she passed…"

She paused as if her friend's passing was still hard for her to talk about "…well, I simply continued on as she'd always done."

"That happens. Sometimes it's hard for a family to step back and see a person's capability. Well, if Liam will let me work with Colm—that's why I'm here."

"Oh, he'll let you. I might not be his mother, or even related by blood, but I'm as close as the boys have to a relative, and I have some clout. I'll use it on your behalf." Mrs. Taylor's bravado seemed at odds with her dimpled smiles.

"Thank you, Mrs. Taylor."

Mrs. Taylor reached across the table and patted her hand. "Now, you call me Aunt Betty. Everyone does. And you tell me what you need from Liam, and I'll see to it that you get it. I can't tell you how much I've worried about Colm. I'm not getting any younger and I don't know what Liam will do when I'm gone."

"Mrs. Taylor—"

The woman gave her a look and Anna hastily amended, "Aunt Betty. I'm sure you'll be here for a long time, but I really think there's a whole world of opportunities for

Colm, and I'd like to show them to him, if his brother permits me to."

"Like I said, you don't worry about Liam. I'll take care of him. When do you want to start?"

"Tomorrow morning at eight?"

"That sounds great to me. We'll see you then."

Colm was busily putting the dishes in the dishwasher.

"Colm, would it be okay if I came over again tomorrow?" Anna asked.

He turned around and grinned. "Oh, yeah. We can finish our buildin'."

"Sure we can. And maybe we could try a few other things, too."

"Okay, that'd be good, Anna." He hugged her goodbye and Anna didn't mind his wet hands as she hugged him back. "Yeah, I'll see ya tomorrow, Anna."

LIAM OPENED the front door for Anna the next morning.

"*Mr. Franklin,*" she said, obviously surprised. "Sorry, I was expecting Mrs. Taylor."

"I'm home today. I wanted to be home yesterday, but I had a meeting, otherwise you'd have dealt with me."

He loved working for himself, except days like yesterday, when he wished he had an employee to send to meetings.

Because his work centered around computers and programming, he was able to do a lot of it online from his home office, but sometimes he had to see customers in person. Thankfully, yesterday's meeting had been with a small firm in town. It had been one of his first clients. Thanks to the Internet, he now did security work for businesses all over the country. Those face-to-faces weren't just an afternoon out of the office, which is why he'd found himself at The Sunrise Foundation.

He reminded himself that he made a good living and was able to be at home most days.

Still, he wished he had been here because he'd have saved himself Aunt Betty's tongue-lashing. She'd told him that Anna was coming back to work with Colm to be more self-sufficient, and his less-than-enthusiastic response had started the lecture. Every concern he voiced only made it worse.

"I'm sorry you couldn't join us." Anna's expression didn't quite match her words. Though her look was quickly replaced by an all-business one that Liam recognized because he'd used it himself with difficult customers.

"Well, I'm glad you're here today," she said with what sounded like forced enthusiasm. "Maybe we can talk for a few minutes?"

"Come in." He led her into the living room and gestured to one of the chairs. He took the other one opposite her.

"You have a beautiful home," she said conversationally. "And that porch. I really love the porch. It makes the house seem so friendly and approachable."

"This is my parents' house. I grew up here and moved back in after they passed away. I thought the continuity was important for Colm, given the circumstances."

"I'm sorry. Mrs. Taylor said that's when she started helping you out. I'm glad you had some support. But still, I'm sorry for your loss."

He didn't say anything to that, because Liam didn't know what to do with sympathy. He remembered standing at the funeral home while a long line of his parents' friends filed by expressing their own sorrow and empathizing with his. He'd nodded woodenly, and tried not to envy Colm's ability to hug everyone.

Needing to change the subject, he said, "So, about my brother?"

"I'd like to spend some time with Colm. A couple of hours a few times a week. Mrs. Taylor seemed to think you'd be okay with that."

Liam couldn't help but smile. "That was a polite way of saying that Aunt Betty threatened to kick my butt if I didn't let you work with him."

Anna laughed and the movement sent her myriad of curls bouncing every which way, just like when they'd met. Again, Liam wanted to reach out and touch them. They were like a living entity, moving as she spoke. But being attracted to Anna was the last thing he needed, so he kept his hands at his sides.

She was still chuckling as she said, "Yes, I believe there was some promise on her part of using threats if necessary. I'd really like it not to be necessary, Mr. Franklin. I think I have something to offer your brother. I think Colm can do a lot more than you believe."

"I won't see him upset or hurt. I don't want him pushed into doing things he's not comfortable with. I've worked very hard to keep a routine for him since my parents died." Liam felt a lump in his throat at the thought of their passing. There was a sense of finality—the knowledge that his father would never realize that Liam's *tinkering with computers* was indeed turning into a successful business.

His parents had been in their forties when they'd had him and Colm, and his father had some very old-world attitudes about what constituted real work. He'd looked at Liam's start-up company as an unnecessary risk. He pointed out that Liam could make more money and have more security working for an already established company. But Liam liked working for himself. He liked the autonomy. And his decision to start his own company had paid off. Liam desperately wished his father could know.

"Mr. Franklin, was Colm upset yesterday after he served us our snack and then cleaned up?"

"No," he admitted. His brother had been excited when Liam had come home last night, telling him that he could make his own snacks now. Someone didn't have to do it for him. "No, he wasn't upset at all."

"Great. Then if you don't mind, I'd like to keep going—see what else Colm can do for himself. I'll be by mornings for now, but that's subject to change. And I'll look for someone who can stay with him when you have to travel."

"What do you think Colm needs to be doing for himself, Ms. Chapel?" He bristled at the implication that somehow his parents hadn't helped Colm enough—his mother had devoted her life to his brother. He was about to say as much to Ms. Chapel but she started talking, and as at their first meeting, he realized that when Ms. Chapel started talking, it was like a speeding freight train. Unstoppable.

"Listen, Mr. Franklin, Colm is a wonderful, well-adjusted man. And I know that's because of what your family gave him—a stable, loving home. But…" She paused.

"But," she started again, "everyone needs new challenges. I think I can give that to Colm. Challenge him. Help him grow."

"And I can't?" he asked.

"You can—and I'm hoping you'll help."

"And what about additional help?"

"Let me know the dates that Mrs. Taylor can't cover for you and I'll organize someone."

It rankled, asking this woman for help. A very big part of Liam wanted to tell her never mind, he'd arrange it on his own. He wanted to assure her that he and Colm were fine as is. But even as he thought the words, he realized it was a lie. He did need help.

So, as much as he hated to say it, he agreed. "Fine."

At that moment, Anna Chapel smiled.

Other than her wild hair, he'd thought there was nothing especially remarkable about her. Which is why he couldn't quite figure out why she seemed beautiful. Each of her features was decidedly average, but put together, they made Anna striking.

And that particular revelation made Liam feel even more uncomfortable than before.

"Thanks, Mr. Franklin. Do you mind if I go find Colm now?"

"No, make yourself at home, Ms. Chapel." The words sounded polite enough, but Liam knew that his tone must have been less than inviting, because the woman frowned, then sighed.

"I will, Mr. Franklin. I will."

TWO HOURS LATER, Anna said, "Okay, Colm that's it for today. I'll see you tomorrow, though."

"I'll be ready for you, Anna. All by myself. 'Cause I can do it, just like I can make snacks. Ya think I can do other things, Anna?"

"I think you can do lots of things, Colm."

Today they'd concentrated on the basics. Colm had been completely sheltered by his family. Someone laid out his clothes. Someone made his bed. Someone prepared his breakfast then did his dishes.

Colm Franklin was able to do all those jobs himself, and the more time she spent with him, the more she was convinced that Colm could do many others as well.

"Come on, Anna, I'll take you to the door," Colm said. "'Cause that's what a gentleman does. Mommy told me. *You be nice to the ladies, Colm.* And I was. I always opened the door for her, and I pushed in her chair at the table, too."

"That was sweet. Though I can push in my own chair."

"I think she coulda, too." He laughed. "My mommy was a funny woman, but she was nice and smiled a lot. Like you do, Anna. And tomorrow you'll be back, right?"

The compliment touched her. "Thank you, Colm. That was sweet. And yes, I'll be back tomorrow. I won't be able to come every day, but I'll try to be here a lot of days, okay?"

"And you'll teach me stuff?" he asked again.

"Yes, I'll teach you as much as you want me to."

He frowned a little. "What if I goof up?"

"Remember what I said yesterday?"

He nodded vigorously. "If you spill the milk, you'll wipe it up. If you drop the cookies, you pick them up. If you make a mess, clean it up," he parroted.

"That's right. Everyone makes a mess sometimes."

"But not Liam—he's smart."

"Even Liam. Even me. Even Aunt Betty."

Colm laughed as if she had to be teasing him. "Nuh-uh."

"Everyone, Colm. Everyone makes mistakes. Everyone has accidents and makes a mess. All you can do is do your best to clean it up and fix it afterwards."

"But I make lots of mistakes."

"Hey, it might take you a little longer to learn something, but you learn it. We'll keep going over it until you know it."

"Even if it takes a lot of times?" he asked.

"Even if."

"And you won't get mad?" he checked.

"Not even a little."

Quickly, he engulfed her in his arms. "I love you, Anna."

She hugged him back.

"So, how did it go?" Liam asked, approaching them.

Colm let go of Anna, turned around and immediately hugged his brother. "It was good, Liam. Anna's teachin' me to do stuff for myself, but it don't matter if I make mistakes, 'cause she says we'll clean it up, right, Anna?"

She wasn't sure why, but watching Colm hug Liam and prickly Liam return the hug, Anna had a Hallmark-commercial reaction. A warm, mushy, on-the-verge-of-tears sort of feeling. She kept it at bay, sure that Liam would disapprove. "Right, Colm, we'll clean it up."

Liam clapped his brother on his shoulder. "So, bud, you'll have to show me what you learned today after Anna leaves."

"It's better stuff than I learned in school. See ya tomorrow, Anna." Colm waved then ran up the stairs.

Liam watched Colm disappear, then turned to Anna and asked, "What do you suppose he's up to?"

"If I were going to guess, he's making his bed, again. He mentioned he was going to like going to bed tonight because he'd have made the bed himself. And if his enjoyment goes up incrementally each time he makes it, he's going to officially have the best night's sleep ever."

"He can make his own bed?"

She nodded. "He's a special man, Mr. Franklin. I've left you some papers to read through about my teaching strategy for Colm. Goals. The criteria for taking new steps. It's all there. If you have any concerns, let me know. I'll see you both tomorrow."

Liam stood in the doorway and watched

Anna Chapel get in her car. For a moment, she stared wistfully at the house, and he wondered what she was thinking. Then she started her tiny gray car and took off down the road.

Liam paused, letting the knowledge that Colm was upstairs making his bed sink in.

It sounded like such a simple thing, but it wasn't simple at all. Now, Liam speculated as to what other kinds of things his brother could do. Things he'd never been given a chance to do because no one had thought he could.

No one but Anna Chapel.

ANNA AND COLM fell into an easy routine over the next few weeks as April progressed and spring settled more firmly into place. A couple of hours a day, three or four times a week if she was able, she and Colm practiced tasks together. Only it wasn't really a job in Anna's mind, it was a delight. Anna truly enjoyed all her clients, but Colm soon became a very special one. He was always open to trying something new, and found such joy when he'd mastered the skill. This week's goals involved cooking.

Since pouring those first glasses of milk, Colm had been building a set of kitchen skills: making peanut butter and jelly sandwiches, getting snacks, rinsing dishes. The man who'd never been encouraged to do kitchen work had discovered he loved it. So this week, they were trying actual cooking.

Colm's first solo meal was spaghetti. Anna sat on a stool and offered advice and listened as Colm's excitement bubbled over. "Liam's gonna be surprised, huh, Anna?"

"Very surprised."

He wiped his hands on the front of the apron he was wearing, then opened a cupboard and took out a large bowl.

"Liam liked my waffles the other day. But ya don't really cook those."

"Hey, you used a toaster," Anna reminded him.

"That's toastin', not cookin'." He shook his head as if he was surprised that Anna didn't recognize the difference.

"You're right, toasting's not cooking." She scooched her stool a little closer to the stove.

"But today, it's really cookin' 'cause there's a flame."

The timer rang and Colm clapped his hands. "Are they done?"

"Let's see," Anna said. "Carefully use the spoon and pull one noodle out." She watched proudly as, with the care of a surgeon operating, Colm lifted a noodle from the pot with painstaking slowness.

"Now, you have two options for seeing if it's done. You can taste it, and if it's not hard, it's done, or you can throw it on the wall and if it sticks, it's done."

"Throw food at the wall?" Colm's voice was filled with what might have been shock, but he wore a smile that said the idea was intriguing.

"I don't recommend throwing food as part of your regular cooking technique, and you do have to wipe the wall off when you're done, but if the noodle sticks, you know it's—" As she squeaked out the word, *done,* Colm threw the noodle at the wall with such force that Anna worried that it was going to leave a permanent mark.

"Done!" Colm announced.

"I see that. Okay, now we need to get the noodles out of the water, so—"

The sound of the front door being opened

and closed could be heard, soon Liam came into the kitchen and his eyes immediately honed in on Colm. "Hey, how are things, bud?"

"I'm cookin' dinner tonight. Aunt Betty, she went home early 'cause me and Anna are cookin', and I threw food on the wall, only it's okay 'cause I'll clean it after, but now you gotta go so I can finish. Go. Go."

It was a long sentence that Colm somehow managed to get out in one breath.

"I can take a hint," Liam said, laughing. The laughter died though as he glanced Anna's way. He gave a brisk nod of greeting and said, "Call me if you need help, Ms. Chapel."

"She won't," Colm assured his brother. "Me and Anna are a team, right, Anna?"

"Right, Colm. We've got it under control, Mr. Franklin. Dinner will be ready in a few minutes."

Liam started to leave the room, and Anna called out, "Mr. Franklin, do you think that maybe we could drop the formal address and go with Liam and Anna from now on?"

He turned, frowned, then nodded. "Fine, *Anna*. Let me know if you need me." He turned to go.

"We will, *Liam,*" she called after him.

It had been weeks since she'd begun assisting Colm, but Liam still treated her as if she were an enemy…someone to be on his guard around. She didn't like it, and wasn't sure what she could do about it. She sighed.

Colm didn't notice. He reached for some pot holders and said, "Okay, Anna, let's get us some spaghetti."

She helped Colm with the rest of the meal prep. They'd already made the salad, and after draining the noodles, Colm sliced the bread. Anna talked about safety, warning of the dangers of hot water and sharp knives.

Colm repeated her rules back to her again and again until they set the food on the table.

Anna surveyed the result and was pleased. "Everything's beautiful, Colm. Why don't you go get Liam."

"Liii-ammm," Colm screamed.

She stifled a chuckle and used her best teacher voice. "Colm, what are the rules about inside voices?"

"It's not polite to yell, so we use a quiet inside voice."

"Right. If you go into the living room and get your brother, you don't have to shout."

"Okay." He headed toward the door, but it opened and Liam was standing there. "Hey, see, Anna, the scream worked."

"Yes, but it's not polite." She looked at Liam, who was frowning. So, what had she done now? Working with Colm was so satisfying. His brother? Not so much. More like a pain in her proverbial…

"It looks good, bud," he said to Colm. His genuine pleasure over his brother's successes robbed her of her annoyance.

Anna smiled at Colm. "Well, I'll leave you two to dinner. Now, Colm, when you're done, you help with the dishes, too."

"And wash the wall," Colm said.

"Yes," she agreed, "and wash the wall. I'll see you the day after tomorrow."

"No, Anna!" Colm yelled, stopping Anna in her tracks.

"Inside voice," she reminded him gently. "Is there a problem, Colm?"

He nodded. "Yeah, you helped make the food, you get to eat it."

She glanced at Liam who was actively

scowling at the thought. "No, you made the dinner for your brother," she tried.

"And you," he repeated stubbornly.

"No, sweetie. My job is helping you learn things, things that will make your life and your family's life better. Tonight, we cooked, and you need to share that with your family—with your brother."

"And you," he insisted. "You had a snack with me first time I made it."

Anna didn't know how to get around that, so she looked at Liam, silently asking him for some help.

"Maybe Anna's got a date," Liam said.

Colm chortled. "Nah, she ain't gotta date."

Ouch. She didn't have a date, but still—ouch.

"I think I should be insulted," she said, quietly. And Liam quite unexpectedly laughed. Not a forced laugh either. This was the first real sign that Liam Franklin had a mood other than guarded or grouchy.

As he chuckled, Anna saw another side of the gruff man. A softer side. A side she'd glimpsed when he hugged Colm in the past, but this time it was directed at her, and it was sweet.

"If you don't have a date, *Anna,*" he said her name as if it was still foreign to his lips, "we'd be happy to have you share Colm's first official solo meal."

Part of Anna wanted to lie and make up some excuse why she needed to leave, but instead, she nodded. "I'd love to. Though you know what this means, Colm? You need to set another place at the table."

He broke out in a grin. "Another place for Anna. Got it."

He ran across the kitchen, grabbed a plate and started to run back when Anna called out, "Walk, Colm. We don't want you to fall and get hurt."

"Or break the plate. But if I broke it, it'd be okay, 'cause we'd clean it up, right, Anna?"

He was so attentive, remembering her comments and instructions. "Right, Colm."

When he'd set the plate on the table, he ran and got one butter knife and slowly walked toward the table.

"Uh, why don't we sit down?" Liam suggested. "It looks as if this may take a while."

He pulled out one of the chairs from the small kitchen table.

Anna was surprised by the act of chivalry. She'd never been a woman who insisted on such things. She was more than capable of pulling out her own chair or opening a door. But she didn't find having a guy do them offensive, either. She simply hadn't expected such a gesture from Liam Franklin. Wasn't she still the enemy?

She took the seat and as Liam gently nudged her chair into the table, his hand brushed against her back. There was no bolt of lightning but there was suddenly an awareness for Anna. She'd only ever seen Liam as a—well, a barrier. Yet here, now, as he took his seat and smiled as Colm carefully set a place for her at the table, she again saw the man who cared deeply about his brother.

"Thank you," she said.

"You're welcome."

They sat in silence until it became uncomfortable, but were saved when Colm finished and took his seat. "So let's eat!"

He dished some pasta onto his plate enthusiastically and passed the bowl to Anna, who took some and passed it to Liam. The salad and rolls went around in a similar fashion. Anna found herself waiting for Liam to take his first bite. He smiled and said, "Very good, Colm."

"Yeah, it is." Colm's mouth was full of food, so his words were a bit difficult to understand, but his smile wasn't.

That smile was what made Anna's job so rewarding. There was a pride in it that showed Colm's growing realization that he could, as Sunrise promised, lead an exceptional life. That's what she wanted for Colm Franklin—an exceptional life.

After they'd finished eating, Colm announced, "I'm done," and made for the door.

"Uh-uh, Colm," Anna called. "You cooked, so you get to help clean up."

"Oh." A moment later, he brightened. "Okay, Anna. I can do that."

"First we clear the table. The leftovers go in a container in the fridge and…"

She didn't expect Liam to stay and help, and when he did, she wasn't sure what to make of it. He kept giving her odd looks, and she had even less understanding of what they were about.

"Kitchen's done," Colm said loudly half an hour later. "I'm gonna go watch TV. I think my Wizard show is on Disney. Anna, you wanna watch it with me?"

She glanced at Liam who was frowning. "I should probably be leaving, Colm."

"Not yet, Anna," Colm said. "You could stay longer, 'cause you have no date, remember?"

She expected Liam to agree that it was time for her to go home. She was sure he'd be polite. He'd make some noise about how he was sure she had something else to do. But what he said was, "Maybe we could all play a game? If you have the time, Anna." He seemed to say her name with more ease.

Colm grabbed her hand. "Yeah, Anna, that'd be good. We can play a game."

Anna smiled. "Maybe a hand of Go Fish?"

"I don't know that one," Colm said.

"If you can find some cards, I can teach you." She'd barely got the words out when Colm shot down the hallway toward the living room.

"Are you sure Colm can handle a card game?" Liam asked.

"Liam, he can count and read a lot of words. It might take him a while to get the feel for the game, but he'll do fine."

And he did. Within a couple of hands, Colm had the idea and was holding his own.

"Go fish!" he shouted gleefully.

Anna did and on Colm's next turn, he put all his cards down. "I got 'em. You gave me that five and I got it."

"Great job, Colm." She glanced at her watch. "But now, I really need to get home. I have an early day tomorrow."

"You have an early day here tomorrow?" Colm asked.

"No. We talked about this, remember? We marked the calendar in the kitchen. I'm back the day after tomorrow."

Colm threw his arms around her and hugged her tightly. "Okay. I'll miss you, Anna, 'cause you teach me lots of stuff, like making spaghetti and puttin' stuff in the fridge after we're done eatin'. You teach me good."

"I taught you—"

He interrupted. "Yep, you did."

Liam was smiling—again. Anna thought she could easily get used to seeing that expression on his face. He said, "Get your shower and put your pajamas on, bud. I'll show Anna out."

"Okay. 'Night, Anna." Colm hugged her again.

She mussed his hair. "'Night, Colm."

She knew from Liam's tone that he wanted to talk to her, so she waited until Colm disappeared up the stairs and said, "Yes?"

He didn't look annoyed, but if not, she wasn't sure what he wanted to talk about.

He simply said, "Thank you."

"For…?"

"For everything. You were right. Colm is capable of so much more than I ever imagined."

His admission surprised and touched her. "You're welcome."

"Anna, I have to go out of town on Thursday. I know that three days is short notice, but it's only one night, and I wondered if you'd found someone to stay with Colm?"

Anna had put off confirming someone. She wasn't sure why, but had a sneaking suspicion that it was because she didn't want to share the Franklin brothers with anyone else. "If you don't mind, maybe I'll stay with him? I mean, it's one night, and it would give us more time to work together. I see so much potential in Colm, and there doesn't seem to be enough time in my day to try as much as I would like to with him."

Liam didn't offer his opinion about her staying with Colm. Instead, he said, "Can I ask you a personal question?"

"You can, but I don't promise to answer." She smiled, hoping to soften her response. Liam was so much more approachable tonight that she didn't want to jinx it.

"Why?" was all he asked.

"Huh?"

"Why do you do what you do? I can't imagine the money is fantastic. And it seems that the hours are long. So, why do you work for Sunrise?"

That was a question that Anna not only didn't mind answering, but relished sharing. Maybe Liam would understand her goals for Colm better if she did.

"I had a client. Denny. He was starting his first job at a local plant where he would be packing boxes. It wasn't only him. I worked with the supervisor, as well. I explained that I'd help Denny get the rhythm of the job down, and stressed that he should do well with the status quo, but that for out-of-the-ordinary things he would require someone to help him. I like being sure that a client's boss has realistic expectations. Two months after I'd gone, Denny's supervisor called and told me that they'd hired a new person and that when the woman had made a mistake on the assembly, Denny had gone over and helped her. He said that Denny had told her that everyone makes mistakes. That she should take her time and ask for help when she needed it. The supervisor was so impressed. He wanted to employ more people from our program."

"Those were your words that Denny said, weren't they? I recognize them from Colm. If you make a mistake, it's like the milk—you clean it up and start over. Things like that."

"Yes." She knew she could be somewhat repetitious with her catch phrases, but her clients needed to hear them over and over until they fully understood them. "And to answer your question, that's why I do it. There are so many special people out there. They might take longer to learn something, or they might need to learn a bit differently than most folks, but with some assistance and time, they can lead remarkable lives. And if I can help that along, well, it means something to me. My job is important to people and that's why I do it."

Even as the words left her mouth, Anna wished she'd said something…well, something less. She felt naked. Exposed. And, Liam Franklin was the last person she wanted to feel like this with.

She wasn't sure why and she wasn't about to explore the reason. "I really should go now. Thanks for allowing me to share Colm's first meal."

"About Thursday," Liam said before she could bolt out the door. "Yes. I knew you'd suggest someone reliable, but I'd have worried. I trust you with Colm. It's a big meeting, and I appreciate you saving me the worry. Thank you."

"You're welcome. I'll be here on Wednesday and you can give me the specifics of your trip then."

"I'll see you day after tomorrow, then."

"Wednesday," she agreed, then rushed out. Admittedly, an annoyed Liam Franklin seemed much easier to deal with than this insightful one.

Anna wasn't sure why.

CHAPTER THREE

"Okay, Li, what gives?" Patrick Yu asked breathlessly on Friday night as Liam got out of his car.

His neighbor pushed his walker at NASCAR-worthy speed toward Liam. Meanwhile, Liam was pulling his suitcase from the backseat, anxious to get in the house, a sense of…he wasn't sure how to define it. Anticipation? Excitement?

He'd talked to Colm on the phone last night, and his brother had seemed fine. More than fine. He'd been excited that Anna was spending a night. "It's like a sleepover, Liam. I never had one of those before, but you used to. Now, it's my turn. Me and Anna are gonna make s'mores, but I don't know what those are, still we're going to make 'em."

Patrick waved a hand in front of Liam's face. "Earth calling Liam."

Liam gave himself a mental shake. "Sorry. How are things, Patrick?"

"Fine. I was asking about the new woman? Actually, I asked what gives, and by that I meant, tell me about your new woman. I'm old and live vicariously through your exploits, which I have to confess, are very few and far between." The elderly man ran his hand through his very thick gray hair, leaving it looking as if the barber had modeled his style after Einstein's.

"She's not my woman," Liam assured his neighbor. "Even if she was, I can't imagine Anna would want to be referred to as my woman."

Patrick chuckled. "Probably not, but I'd never use the term in front of her. I might be old, but I'm not dumb. Women don't take kindly to being called women. I heard some don't even like being referred to as ladies? I'm guessing *gals* and *broads* are off-limit terms, as well. Me, I stick to *people* when women are about. It saves a lot of hassles. But she's not here, so tell me who is she if she's not your new woman? Her car's in your driveway a lot lately. And I couldn't help but notice it was here all night."

"Her name's Anna Chapel, she's with The Sunrise Foundation and she's helping out with Colm. She spent the night here with him while I was in Jackson, Tennessee, for a meeting with a prospective client." He lifted his carry-on bag to emphasize he hadn't been home last night with Anna.

Patrick nodded his approval. "Glad to see you've got some smarts, boy. Now, Mrs. Taylor is a fine woman, but a man your age needs to hire someone younger and easier on the eyes. This girl seems like she'll do."

"It's not like that, Patrick. Anna is here for Colm."

"Then you better see about making it like that. Girls like her don't stay on the shelf for long. And a man your age needs a woman. Believe me, if I had it to do over again, I'd have snagged me a woman a decade or two ago. A man can only sow wild oats for so long, and one day he finds he hasn't sowed enough, so there's no harvest and that gets a mite lonely."

Liam ignored Patrick's comments. "I don't

even know if she's dating someone." Hell, he'd never asked Anna any questions about her personal life. Maybe she *was* married?

He'd never seen a wedding ring, but not everyone wore one. The thought of Anna with a boyfriend or a husband was… Well, it didn't bother him, of course. But if she did have a significant other, then she'd been pretty neglectful, what with all the time she'd spent with Colm and him. He wouldn't like to feel as if he and Colm were to blame if Anna's relationship went south.

"You'd better find out if she's dating. I came out to say thanks for mowing my lawn the other day."

Liam nodded. "You know it's not a problem." Patrick was well beyond an age he should be doing things like that, and it only took Liam twenty minutes to do the elderly man's lawn, too. "That's what neighbors are for."

"You're a nice boy. Now show me you're a smart one and try to land that cute girl." Patrick started back toward his house. "Anna. That's a nice solid name. From Hannah. It means gracious."

Patrick had a *Jeopardy*-worthy knowledge of obscure facts, and Liam didn't doubt his accuracy in pegging the origin of Anna's name. "And my name? What does Liam mean?"

Patrick turned around and raked his hand through his hair, making it stand further on end. Einstein on a very bad hair day. "It's Gaelic, boy. A form of William. It means warrior. Your brother's name is Gaelic, too. It means dove…gentle. I think your mother knew what she was doing when she named you both. Be a warrior, fight for the girl."

"I don't have much time for girls, what with work and Colm, but thanks, Patrick."

"Happy to give you an opinion any time, boy. Not that you listen to me."

No one but Patrick ever referred to him as a boy anymore. To be honest, Liam was hard-pressed to remember a time he'd felt boyish. For as long as he could remember he'd had responsibilities, and he'd had even more since his parents had died.

He opened the door to the sound of laughter that immediately made him forget about responsibility.

"Come on, Anna," Colm said in the living room. "Knock-knock."

"Who's there?" he heard Anna ask.

"Colm, silly."

Anna burst out laughing. It wasn't some fake titter, but a belly laugh that said she really did find his brother amusing.

"Come on, Anna. Your turn. I think I'm winnin' so far."

"Okay, last one. Hey, Colm, knock, knock."

"Who's there?"

"Banana."

"Banana who?"

"Banana Anna, now time for pajamas."

This time Colm was laughing, and Anna joined in. It was a wonderful sound to come home to.

"Hey, knock, knock," Liam called by way of a greeting.

"Liam," Colm screamed and a split second later came barreling into the living room archway. "You're home." He threw himself at Liam. It was apparent that Colm trusted Liam to catch him, and Liam vowed, not for the first time, that he always would.

Colm let him go as abruptly as he'd hugged him. "You bring me somethin'?"

"Maybe."

Colm laughed. "You always bring me something. Come on. Where is it?"

"How about you go put on your pajamas, like Anna said, and I'll find it."

"Okey-dokey." He let go of Liam and ran up the stairs at full speed.

"Walk on the stairs, Colm," Anna called.

Colm slowed, but it was barely perceptible.

"So, how was your trip?" She started to get up off the couch.

"Please, don't go yet," Liam said. Anna sank back down and he sat across from her. It was nice to have someone ask about his trip. He'd never thought about it, but it had been a long time since someone had. "To answer your question, the trip was great. An unqualified success. It's a big account."

Jackson Tech's business would keep his small computer security company in the black for a while.

"Congratulations, Liam. I'm so happy for you."

"And how were things here?"

"Fantastic. Colm did his own laundry." She smiled as if remembering something that pleased her. "Now, when you see how it's folded, don't belittle it. It's not perfect, but a few wrinkles aren't a very high price for the sense of pride he took in the job. He's not quite ready to take over on his own, but he did a good job. If you don't mind taking the time, you should have him help from now on."

Liam felt a surge of guilt at the thought of what Colm had learned and accomplished in the short time he'd been in Anna's company. "I should have worked more with him. I should have pushed Mom to let him try new things. But she was always afraid he'd get hurt, and after a while… Well, I never thought about it. Colm was Colm. And what he did or didn't do was part of him."

"Liam, we've had this discussion before." Anna leaned forward, placing her hands on the coffee table and sending her curls tumbling over her shoulders, as if by getting close enough, she could somehow drive her point home. "You've done a wonderful job with your brother. Colm is well-adjusted and happy. He couldn't learn or accomplish any of these things if he weren't."

"I never knew—"

"And I don't know a thing about computers, and yet you do all sorts of amazing things with them. I find the tangle of machines and monitors up in your office intimidating to look at. You're a good caring man, Liam Franklin. You came to Sunrise for help, you've let me work with Colm. You love him, you care for him. You have nothing to feel guilty about. Nothing."

She looked so sincere. Wanting him to believe that she was willing to fight for him just as she always seemed so willing to fight for Colm.

Liam had a sudden urge to lean over the coffee table in order to close the distance between them…and kiss her. The urge caught him totally unaware. It wasn't that he hadn't noticed that Anna was attractive. Oh, maybe it had taken him a moment or two to notice, but that smile and laugh—he couldn't shake them. And he'd quickly learned to appreciate that she was good at her job—good with his brother. But wanting to kiss her?

The urge was a surprise, and one he wasn't planning to indulge in. Instead, he simply placed his hand on top of one of hers. She didn't pull away, but turned her hand so they were palm to palm. She gave his hand a squeeze, and for a long moment, they both sat silently like that.

Finally, Liam sat back, breaking the connection. "Thanks." His voice felt rough as it maneuvered through his tangle of emotions.

"Anytime." She started to stand. "I should be going."

"Hey, Anna," Colm called from the top of the stairs. "Knock, knock."

"Who's there?" she called back, not bothering to remind him about inside voices.

"Pajama." They could hear him thundering down the stairs.

"Pajama who?" Anna called.

Colm burst into the living room. "Pajamas are on Colm, that's who."

"I think there's a chance he's missed the point," Liam whispered, even though he was laughing as hard as Colm was.

"The point is having fun, so I think he's got it right," Anna whispered back.

"Hey, Anna, wanna play a game of Go Fish?" Colm asked.

"Maybe another time, Colm. Your brother's probably tired. I bet he wants some peace and quiet."

"Nah, Liam'll play, right, Liam?" Very seriously, he turned to Anna. "He's like a superhero and can do anythin'."

What could he say to that look of utter confidence that Colm shot him. "Sure, Colm. That is, if Anna hasn't had enough of us yet."

She gave him a look he couldn't quite read. She slowly answered, "No. I'm not tired of the two of you yet."

"Not never," Colm said. "Anna, she likes me. 'Course, I don't know if she likes you," he teased.

"I like both Franklin brothers," she said diplomatically.

"Nah, she likes me more, 'cause you're a grump," Colm teased. "Anna likes me the best."

Liam knew Colm wanted him to argue about who Anna liked most as another kind of game, but he didn't because that urge to kiss her hadn't completely disappeared, despite his attempts at quashing it.

They all sat down to play Go Fish, and as he watched Colm, he realized that his brother had never been this happy. Sure, he'd been content. Cared for. Cosseted. But since Anna had come into their lives, Colm had really been growing by experiencing new things. He'd been happy in a way he'd never been before.

"Go fish," Colm screamed.

"Inside voice, Colm," Anna said softly.

"Sure, Anna. I forgot. But you know it's okay to forget," he instructed Liam. "Anna says, that's why we got friends to remind us. And after a while we won't forget no more. Inside voice inside. Yep, one day soon I'll remember that on my own."

"Anna's very smart," Liam assured his brother.

"Oh, yeah she is," Colm agreed enthusiastically. "But I bet ya don't know this one, Anna. Knock, knock."

She grinned before Colm could arrive at his punch line.

"Who's there?"

"Inside voice."

"Inside voice, who?"

"Inside voice 'cause screamin' gives Anna a headache."

They both burst into laughter. And despite the fact he knew Colm's knock-knocks didn't quite fit the true essence of the game, Liam laughed as well because, like Colm, he'd been content before, going through the motions at work, at home. But right now, he was more than content. He, too, was happy. Bone-deep happy.

When they finally finished their game, Liam looked at the clock. "Bedtime, bud."

Colm threw himself at Anna and hugged her. "'Night, Anna."

Colm was a hugger. He always had been. His mother used to scold him for hugging strangers. She told him that they didn't like it. Over the years, Colm had eased off on hugging everyone. But Anna never seemed annoyed by Colm's frequent displays of affection. She simply hugged him back. "'Night, Colm."

Colm turned to Liam and hugged him as well. "I liked my sleepover with Anna, but I'm glad you're home."

"Me, too," Liam reassured him.

Colm got to the doorway and turned. "See ya tomorrow, Anna?"

"Sure thing."

"What're we doing tomorrow?"

"It's a surprise."

"I like surprises." He started up the stairs again, then returned and ran full-steam to Liam and hugged him, then sprinted to Anna and hugged her again, too. "'Night." This time they heard him run up the stairs. Then his bedroom door slammed.

Anna gathered up her things. "And now I really need to be going. I'm glad your trip and meeting were a success, Liam. Congrats on the new account."

He followed her into the foyer. "Thank you for staying with Colm. I didn't worry at all. It made concentrating on the business at hand so much easier."

"That's good."

She opened the door, and before she could step onto the porch, Liam asked, "Would you have dinner with me?"

The question came out of the blue just as his previous urge to kiss her had. He felt as surprised as Anna looked as she shut the door again and paused before slowly answering, "Dinner with you…and Colm?"

"No, that's not what I'm asking. Not with Colm. Just you and me. Somewhere other than here, eating something Colm didn't cook."

"To talk about Colm's progress." It was a statement, not a question. Anna sounded as if she'd figured it all out.

And maybe Liam should agree. A meal to talk about Colm. But instead, he said, "No. A date. No talk of Colm allowed."

For the first time since they'd met, Anna Chapel seemed a little less than sure of herself. "A date?"

"Yes, Anna. Unless you're married or have a boyfriend I don't know about. A date. I assume you've been on dates? I'll come pick you up and take you somewhere nice. We'll sit and talk. Get to know each other outside our relationship through Colm."

She was silent for a minute, as if mulling his suggestion over. "Oh."

He should let her off the hook and say, *never mind*, but he pressed on. "Is that a yes, or a no?"

"You're sure you want to have dinner with me? I sort of thought I aggravated you."

"You… Well, you push Colm and push me out of this comfortable little rhythm we've made. Sometimes that's hard for me. I'm responsible for him, and I take that seriously. Making sure Colm's okay, that's always been my job. So, when you push, I worry and I sometimes balk a bit, but even then I don't find you aggravating. Pushy maybe," he teased. "And I'm not asking for a long-term commitment, Anna. It's only one dinner. You and me."

Again she was silent, and finally she nodded. "Sure. Dinner it is."

"Let me check with Aunt Betty and see if she can stay late next Friday. If that works for you?"

She glanced at her wrist, as if to check a watch that wasn't there. "Next Friday. I think I'm free."

"Okay then."

She reached for the doorknob, then stopped and faced him. "Why?"

"Why what?"

"Why would you want to date me? You think I'm pushy and I still suspect that I aggravate you."

"Yes. But you also intrigue me. Mainly, I'd like a date because it's been all I can do not to kiss you tonight."

"Oh."

She turned around, then spun back toward him, stood on tiptoe and kissed him firmly on the lips. Quick, perfunctory. Almost chaste.

It was that *almost* that got him.

Her lips had parted ever so slightly and softened enough to keep the kiss from total chasteness.

Rather than satisfying his need to kiss her, it made Liam want her more.

So, as she sank back onto the flats of her feet, he leaned down and kissed her with the hunger he'd been feeling all night. It was nowhere near chaste. It was carnal.

It was the kind of kiss that normally came much later in a relationship. One that rarely happened before a first date.

Yet, rather than push him away, Anna held on to him, deepening the kiss.

When they parted, she turned one last time and not only opened the door, but hurried out onto the porch. "A date. Yes. I guess that makes sense," she murmured, all but sprinting to her car.

THERE WAS ONLY one word to describe Anna's mood the following Wednesday. Gleeful.

She'd felt that way when Liam had asked her out.

She'd felt that way when she'd kissed him.

She'd felt that way when he'd kissed her back.

And she'd pretty much felt that way every day since.

She'd made sure that Colm's appointment was the last one each day, which meant when Liam asked her to stay she didn't have any conflicting appointments. And he had asked her to stay on the days she worked with Colm. Every time.

Which is why she was with both of the Franklin brothers at the park, sitting next to Liam on a bench, watching Colm on the swing.

"...and then I..." The rest of Liam's sentence was computer gobbledygook. Anna recognized some words like router and modem, but she wasn't sure exactly what a ping was, other than half of a ping-pong table. It didn't matter. She just liked listening to Liam's enthusiastic description of his day.

He laughed. "I did it again, didn't I?"

Anna nodded. "It's okay. I like listening to you."

"Liam, Anna, watch!" Colm cried as he pumped the swing a little higher.

"We're watching," Liam called back. He kept his eyes on his brother as he picked their conversation back up. "I guess I'm not used to having someone to share my day with. I'm going to have to make my conversations less geek-like."

"Or you can teach me the terminology. For instance, what's a ping?"

He looked at her. "Do you mean it?"

"What?"

"You want to learn about computers?"

Anna chuckled. "Well, no. I've never had any driving need to know anything more about computers than how to turn one on, but I do want to know more about you, and you work with them, so I need to know enough to follow a conversation."

"Most of the women I've dated haven't even wanted to know that much," he admitted.

The way he worded it made it sound as if there were tons of women in his past. "Most women?"

"Anna, I have dated. I'll confess, since my parents—since I moved back into the house to take care of Colm, I haven't dated as much, and no one seriously in a long time."

Anna had to admit, this was more interesting than computers. "Sorry. Of course you date. It's just you haven't been on one since I started working with Colm."

"Wrong. I do have a date. Day after tomorrow, as a matter of fact." He smiled, and Anna was struck by how very blue his eyes were. A dark blue that almost matched the evening sky.

She laughed. "Yes, you do have a date on Friday. As it happens, so do I."

"Now, isn't that a coincidence?"

"Yes, it's amazing how life sometimes works out like that."

"So, tell me about this guy you're dating?"

"Oh, he's smart. Knows computers. You two would definitely be able to talk. And…"

"Wow, you're hesitating. I don't know if smart is enough of a recommendation."

Anna knew he was still teasing, but she found herself getting more serious. "No, there's so much more to him. He's caring. You should see how he interacts with his brother. He's all heart." It was true. She could list a lot of qualities about Liam that appealed to her, but the way he cared for Colm was the biggest factor. Wanting to lighten things up, she added in a conspiratorial whisper. "And he's kind of cute."

"Just kind of?" Liam joked.

"Well, maybe more than kind of, but I'm sure I won't mention it to him. I wouldn't want to give him a swollen ego."

She thought he'd keep up their silly banter, but instead, he grew more serious. "And how about you? You haven't mentioned dating anyone."

"I date occasionally, but I've never found anyone that I wanted to go out with more than a few times."

"So…" Liam said.

Anna wasn't sure what to say now. She felt tongue-tied. Thankfully, Colm interrupted what could be a very long pause.

"Hey, you guys! Look at me. I can almost touch the sky with my shoes."

They both directed their attention to Colm trying to touch the sky, and Liam put his arm over her shoulder.

It felt very right there.

"BREATHE, ANNA," Ceelie commanded the following Friday afternoon. They'd attended a seminar and had closed the office for the day. They got to Anna's in time for Ceelie to play fashion consultant before picking up her kids at school. Anna was pulling a variety of outfits from her closet. "Seriously, it's simply a dinner."

"I know," Anna replied. But knowing it, and being calm and zen about it were two very different things. "Being this nervous about a date is ridiculous."

Ceelie shook her head as Anna held up an earth-colored sheath. "It looks like mud. And yes, it is ridiculous. It's not as if you've never gone on a first date before."

"You and I both know I've gone on far too many first dates," she grumbled. "And not nearly as many second ones."

"You're discriminating. If a man doesn't

interest you, you admit it and move on," Ceelie said.

"My mother says that I'm too picky. Of course, my mother firmly believes if he's breathing and male, he has potential." She immediately felt embarrassed. "Sorry. That wasn't kind."

Ceelie shot her a sympathetic look. "Being truthful isn't necessarily unkind, Anna."

"No. But certain truths will never change, so why rail against them? My mom is what she is. And she's right in this case. I am picky. I'd rather be alone than spending time dating for the sake of dating. I want someone who will challenge me, who will support me. I want someone who's…" She hesitated. "Never mind my catalog of dating necessities."

"Do you think Liam could be that someone?" Ceelie asked.

"No idea. That's what a first date is all about." She didn't want to admit that she wasn't sure Liam could ever meet those ideals. But one aspect of a date she hadn't put on her list was she wanted someone she had chemistry with. And though she hadn't noticed it at first, their kiss was combustible, which spoke to more than a smattering of something between them.

They hadn't kissed the whole week, but sitting on a park bench watching Colm on a swing, Liam's arm around her…. Well, it might not have been combustible, but it was definitely sweet.

It was such a little thing, but it made for a moment she'd always remember. Park bench, and all.

She held out her standard first-date dress.

"Ugh. Don't wear that black number. I've always thought you looked like you should be off to a funeral home when you've got that on. Go with some color. The red?"

Anna had no idea why she'd bought that particular dress. It was form-fitting and always left her feeling half-naked. "No. I'd be uncomfortable. Too flashy."

Ceelie rifled through the closet a moment while Anna watched.

"How about this?" Ceelie had pulled out an ice-blue dress.

"You don't think it's a little much?" It wasn't as risqué as the red number, but it wasn't what she thought of as a first-date dress. It had spaghetti straps and a tight bodice that dropped at the waist into a very flowy sort of dress. It was flirty and frivolous. "Really?"

She held it up to herself and checked her reflection in the mirror.

"I think it's just right. Perfect, even." Ceelie glanced at her watch. "I'd better run or else I'll be late. I was late once picking the kids up and I've never heard the end of it. They had to wait *five* whole minutes." Ceelie mimicked her daughter Natalie's dramatic flair perfectly.

"Hurry, then," Anna agreed. "I don't want to be the cause of another trauma like that."

"Have fun tonight, Anna. This doesn't have to be serious. And frankly, it sounds like Liam could use a night off as much as you could."

Anna smiled at Ceelie. "Tick-tock."

"I'm gone." Ceelie rushed from the room.

Anna fingered the material of the soft blue dress. Was it a little much?

Maybe. But this once, she wanted something a little much. She glanced at her watch. Three hours until the date. She had plenty of time to decide.

As if on cue, the phone rang. Anna picked it up.

"Dear, this is your mother," her mother announced, as if Anna might not recognize her mom's voice. Although it had been a few weeks since her mother had called, Anna knew her mother's modus operandi and guessed another boyfriend had dumped her.

Her mother was generally the dumpee, not the dumper. Even in the most hopeless of relationships, Donna Chapel held out hope that it would last. Right up until the minute she was dumped.

Anna fingered the ice-blue dress, before hanging it up in the closet. "Hi, Mom."

"Are you going to ask me how things are?"

Anna obliged. "How are things, Mom?"

"Horrible. I'll be at your door in a minute and I'll tell you all about it."

"Mom, I—" But Anna was talking to a dial tone.

Great. Just great. Moments like this, her mother needed a lot of time and attention. After which, she'd brush Anna off and be searching for the next potential love of her life.

Donna Chapel had optimism down to a science.

The doorbell rang.

Anna opened the door. "I was in my car out front when I called," her mother said by way of a greeting as she brushed by her.

People said they looked alike. Maybe they did. They were of the same height, and Anna didn't need a mirror to recognize the similarities in their features. The most striking difference was her mother's flame-red hair. But Anna knew without the dye her mom's hair would be the same brown shade as her own.

Still there was a major difference. Her mother had this… Well, aura. It drew men like flies. Anna had never had that. Truth be told, she'd never tried to cultivate it. She loved her mom, but she never wanted to live a life like hers. Her mom rode an emotional rollercoaster. Up one day, down the next. Everything depended on the status of her current relationship. Anna preferred a quieter, steadier life.

"I don't have long, Mom," she said gently. "I've got a date tonight."

Her mother smiled through her tears. "I'm glad, darling. I don't think I'm ever going to date again. Men are fickle creatures. One minute they love you and adore you, the next, they're gone."

Anna led her mother into the living room and they both sat down on the couch. "Now, what happened to Herbert, Mom?"

"No, not Herbert, Moose."

"Moose?" Anna wasn't sure she'd heard about Moose.

"Herbert and I broke up weeks ago at the bar, but I met Moose that same night, and I thought I'd finally found the one. My one. A happily-ever-after sort of man."

Anna wasn't sure that a man named Moose sounded like a happily-ever-after sort of man, but maybe she was prejudiced against men named after animals. She was pretty sure she'd feel the same about a man named Wolf, Horse or Hippo. How about Buck? Would a guy named Buck stick around? She didn't think so.

She realized her mother was waiting for some kind of response. "I'm sorry, Mom." And she was. She was sorry her mother put herself through this time after time.

"I really thought he was it," her mother whispered.

"Really sorry, Mom."

"I know you are, baby." Her mother reached for the box of tissues that only came out when she visited after a break-up or when Anna had a cold.

"Maybe we could get a chick flick and watch it tonight?" her mom asked, the tissue covering the lower half of her face.

"I've got a date, remember?"

Her mom blew her nose, then smiled. "That's right. Tell me all about him."

"It's a first date. No ever-afters in sight. Only two people eating dinner together."

"Oh, a first date. I love first dates. They're so full of potential. You spend time talking and getting to know each other." Her mother sighed. "I really do love first dates. And I'll probably never have one again. Moose was it for me. I'm done. I'll never find my happily-ever-after now."

As much as Anna wanted to assure her mother there was no such thing as a happily-ever-after, that if people were really lucky, sometimes they found a happily-right-now, she stared at her mom. Yes, people might say they looked alike, but Anna's mom was a dreamer. And Anna? She was a realist. She believed in what was here, right now, right in front of her. She didn't rule out falling in love, but she wasn't sure she bought the idea of a soul mate.

"Mom, you know you're not done looking. You believe in your soul mate too much to do that."

"And you, my little Anna, don't."

Her mother stopped crying and she could almost see her mulling over ways to convince Anna there was such a thing as true love.

"No, I don't believe in soul mates," she said gently. "So how about if you dream for both of us?"

"Maybe you should dream a bit. Maybe tonight's first date is the first of many? The start of a lifetime together?"

"Tell you what, if you promise not to sit around at home and mope, then I'll promise to try to dream, at least a little, tonight."

"Well, there is a dance at the club tonight." Her mother paused, then laughed. It was a slight, tinkling sort of sound that once again held a belief that anything was possible.

Anna laughed along with her, because she loved her mother. Oh, her mom drove her crazy, and her quest for one magical relationship that would make her whole always made

Anna think of Don Quixote battling wind-mills. But the truth of it was, Anna appreci-ated that her mother fell so wholeheartedly into things.

"The dance at the club sounds perfect," Anna said. "Don't stay out so late that you can't get up for work tomorrow."

"Oh, about that." Her mother waved her hand. "I have a new job. No more weekends for me."

Anna couldn't help it, she laughed again. Her mother held on to her jobs only a little longer than she held on to her men. "So where do you work now?"

"Near Keller's Market. They put in that new cafeteria. I'm waiting tables and working the register. It's good money, and it's weekdays."

"I'm happy for you, Mom."

"Thanks, sweetie." Her mom leaned forward and kissed her forehead. "Now, I'd best let you get ready for that date. Thanks for rescuing me from the depths of my despair."

"I don't think Moose was worth any real despair."

Her mother, only minutes ago in tears at

the thought of losing Moose, laughed again. "You're right. There are other fish in the sea, aren't there?"

"Yes. And there are plenty of moose in the forest." Oh, that was bad. Anna knew it was, but she grinned regardless.

"Why, Antonia Mary Chapel, was that a joke? My oh-so-serious daughter is teasing me and joking?"

She thought of Colm. "Well, I've been hanging out with this very funny guy lately."

"Maybe I should stay a bit longer so you can tell me all about him?" Her mother studied her. "Is this Mr. Date tonight?"

"No, I'm not dating Mr. Funny Guy. I'll tell you all about my date later. Right now, you should go get ready for the dance and let me get ready for the date."

"The first date." Her mother sighed another wistful sigh.

Anna nodded, wishing she felt better about it. Dating a client's brother wasn't very smart to begin with. She wasn't sure why she'd said yes.

"I hope it's great, honey." Her mom gave her a kiss on the cheek and departed.

Anna quickly took a shower, tried to tame her crazy hair and finally admitted defeat and threw it into a twist. It looked semi-neat for a few seconds, then one of the millions of curls sprang free. She told herself that a slightly messy look was in vogue, though she didn't believe her own lie. She slipped on the ice-blue dress and a pair of heels.

Then waited.

And waited.

She checked the clock and realized that she hadn't waited long, but time seemed to be moving at a different speed. Slower.

Ten minutes after six, the doorbell rang and she felt an overwhelming sense of relief. He hadn't stood her up.

Not that she'd really thought he would. Still, given the odd sense of nerves she had over this date she hadn't been sure.

Anna swung the door open. Liam and Colm were both there.

"Hi, Anna! Aunt Betty got sick and so she couldn't come, and so I'm going to date you, too. Liam wanted to go to some fancy restaurant. I wanna go to Sara's at the beach. They got good burgers there. But Liam says you get to pick, so what d'ya think? Burgers at Sara's?" he wheedled.

Liam shot her a look of apology. But rather than feeling disappointed, Anna felt relieved. She knew how to interact with Liam and Colm, but with Liam on her own, she'd felt unsure and nervous.

She grinned. "Sara's sounds perfect. And afterward, maybe we could take a walk on the beach. But I should go change."

Colm gave her an appraising look and frowned. "Yeah, you hurry and change. You look weird in a dress."

"She looks lovely," Liam said quietly.

Again, Anna could see the apology in his eyes, and reached out and gave his hand a squeeze to say it was fine.

"Just a minute and I'll be right back."

"I'll count," Colm said helpfully, "and see how long it takes you. One. Two…"

Anna laughed because Colm looked so earnest and Liam looked so chagrined. "I'm hurrying," she said for Colm's sake, and added for Liam's, "This is going to be fun."

She wasted no time changing into a pair of khaki capris and a T-shirt. Pulling the shirt over her head loosened the bun, so she pulled her curls into a ponytail. The wind at the beach would wreak havoc on her hair.

She slipped on her sandals and hurried back into the living room.

"I ran out of numbers," Colm said. "That means you was way slow."

"Hey, bud, a gentleman never comments on how long a lady takes to get ready. Even if she is *way slow,*" Liam teased.

Anna enjoyed this playful Liam. Despite the change in plans, she was looking forward to the evening.

LIAM WASN'T the least bit surprised that Anna took Colm coming along on the date so well.

The drive into Erie had gone faster than it normally did. Of course, there were moments when he felt more like a referee than a date. Like over Colm and Anna's mock-squabble about who rode shotgun. Liam declared that dates always won, and they'd both laughed.

That seemed to be the theme of the time they spent with Anna. Laughter.

She had already taught Colm so much, and

she did it with kindness, humor and an under-current of joy.

Sara's burgers were out of this world, and Liam commented on the fact that he'd never seen any one person eat as many French fries as Colm had managed to.

To which his brother responded, "I always got room for fries."

After dinner, they had ice cream cones. Then Liam parked at the Stull Center, and they ate their ice cream as they walked up the beach. Colm darted in and out of the waves, searching for beach glass.

"I'm sorry about the date," Liam said. "This isn't what I planned. Although I had planned on a walk on the beach to watch the sunset. But I thought we'd start with a nice dinner at Joe Root's."

"Life is never quite what we plan, but sometimes those unexpected paths are even better than the ones we'd intended to take."

"You're a philosopher, Anna Chapel."

She shook her head. "No, I'm a realist."

"You can tell yourself that, if it makes you happy, but you are so much more. In fact, you're a dreamer."

"My mother and I were discussing that earlier. She's the dreamer. She always believes there's something wonderful around the next corner. I try to concentrate on what I have in front of me. But tonight, she wanted me to dream a bit, too, so maybe that's what you're sensing."

"You don't think you're a dreamer?" Liam could see that she didn't. That in all sincerity Anna believed what she believed. "I hate to break it to you, Anna Chapel, but you are the Don Quixote of dreams."

She pointed up the beach at the small windmill by the Stull Center. "When I was talking to Mom I made that same comparison…she's Don Quixote. I'm Aldonza. I see things the way they are. No tilting windmills for me. The one over here is as close as I come."

"You can tell yourself that, but I know the truth. You saw in Colm so much more potential than I ever did. You didn't accept the status quo. You—"

"I think we need to change the subject," she said, her discomfort evident.

"Hey, Anna, look at this one." Colm thrust a piece of beach glass into her hand.

She held it up and admired it. "It's beautiful, Colm." She tried to hand it back.

"Nah, it's for you," he said as he darted to the shoreline.

She turned the glass over in her hand.

"You don't like hearing praise, do you?" Liam asked.

"I like action, not words. Speaking of action, I've got to meet with the zoning board on Monday and I'm not sure if I can make my afternoon session with Colm. Is it a problem if I come late?"

"Anna, you're welcome whenever you want." They continued their stroll, and he asked, "So, what's the zoning thing about?"

"Sunrise bought a house. We've got two other group homes in Whedon, and this will be our third. But we need it rezoned to allow a group home. Whedon has a statute on the books that says no more than two unrelated people can live together in a residential house."

They sat on a giant driftwood log as Colm continued his beach-glass hunt and the sun started to set. Anna resumed talking about zoning and group homes.

Liam's hand rested on the log a fraction of

an inch from hers and slowly, he moved it until his pinkie touched hers. It was the smallest of gestures, but he liked it. As he listened to Anna and she told him about the plans Sunrise had for the house—her plans for it—Liam knew he was right. She was lying to herself when she said she was a realist.

Whether or not she really knew it, Anna Chapel was a dreamer of the nth degree.

And for the first time in a long time, Liam felt himself begin to dream a little, and that dream included Anna Chapel.

CHAPTER FOUR

"WHAT'RE WE DOIN' today, Anna?" Colm asked on a Thursday morning two weeks after Anna's almost-solo date with Liam.

Since then, they'd gone out to two more dinners and a movie. It felt normal to have Colm come along. Some women might protest, but to Anna, Colm was such a big part of Liam's life and hers that it seemed right.

"I thought we'd take lunch to Liam. He has a meeting downtown and we could join him afterward."

"Are we gonna buy it? Maybe at Macky's? They got good burgers there. And really good fries. I like fries. With lots of ketchup," he told her.

Anna knew a not-so subtle hint when she heard one, but today's excursion wasn't only a chance for her to see Liam. It was another lesson for Colm. At least if she made it a lesson for Colm, she could rationalize her growing need to see Liam. "I thought it might be more special if you made it. We could eat in the park."

It was a beautiful May day. Warm and sunny. Western Pennsylvania's winters were long, and early springs were soggy. Today was the kind of day everyone dreamed of in January.

"The park is nice. And Liam'd probably think it was real good if I cooked it. What should I make?"

"I thought we'd try egg salad. So, first, you've got to boil some eggs. Let's start by filling a pan with water…"

Anna talked Colm through hard-boiled eggs, and after he had finished the egg salad and put it in the fridge to cool, she helped him bake brownies. While the brownies were in the oven, they cut some carrot sticks and talked about good nutrition.

It was eleven-thirty when Colm had packed a bag with their lunch. "Okay, Anna, let's go. I got shotgun, 'cause you're driving."

"Let's try something else. Today, let's ride a bus."

"A bus?"

She nodded as they walked toward the nearest bus stop. Whedon was so small, it only had two routes for the entire community. And there was a bus that ran into Erie three times a day.

Learning to use public transportation was an important part of Colm's independence. If he could get around town, he could get a job, and someday maybe live on his own.

And in Anna's mind, equipping Colm to live independently, in a house like the Trudy Street one she'd bought for Sunrise recently, was her goal.

Actually, Gilly and Josh, two of the three intended residents of Trudy Street, would be a nice fit for Colm. She'd been discussing the third resident with Ceelie, but they hadn't made up their minds.

Could Colm be ready for a house of his own this year?

Anna never broached the idea with Liam of Colm moving into a group home someday, mainly because they'd been getting along so well and she didn't want to upset the status quo. It was cowardly, and she knew it. She vowed that she'd talk to Liam about it soon.

But for now, they were going to meet him for lunch.

"You need to find one of the bus stops…"

She gave Colm a 101 on the bus system as they waited at the stop. She handed him the proper change. "Now, when the bus driver opens the door, we'll get on and you'll put the money in the little box."

"All by myself, right, Anna?" he checked.

"Right, Colm."

"Liam's gonna be so surprised that we're bringin' him lunch and that I rode a bus. I never rode a bus before, except for school, and I didn't have to pay for that. The bus driver, he'd open the door and say 'Hi, Colm' and I'd always try to sit at the front, 'cause if I sat in the back sometimes kids picked on me. I didn't care 'cause Mommy always said sticks and stones can break your bones but names can never hurt you. But Liam, he cared. He beat some guys up once 'cause they called me a bad name. He got kicked off the bus for a long time, and Mommy drove us to school, but then they let us on again and we rode the bus, and I went back to sitting in the front 'cause the bus driver didn't let those kids call me names and he didn't need to beat them up. That's good, 'cause if the bus driver got kicked off, who'd drive the bus?" Colm laughed at his question.

Anna smiled along with him, but inside, her heart was breaking. And not only for Colm, who had to deal with people who called him names, but for Liam, who'd been kicked off the bus for defending his brother.

She wondered how many fights Liam had been in over the years on Colm's behalf?

"Hey, Anna, you're not gonna fight anyone if they call me names, right? 'Cause I don't want you to get a black eye like Liam did. Only it wasn't black. It was kinda purple, then turned green, so I don't know why you call it a black eye, but you do."

"No, Colm, I'm not going to get a black eye. If someone calls you a name, I'll feel sorry for them because I'll know that their hearts are way too tiny and that must hurt."

"Do ya think I got a tiny heart?" He thumped his own chest. "'Cause it don't hurt, except when Liam's sad because of me, or when Mommy and Daddy died."

"Colm, I'm not a doctor, but I can guarantee, you've got one of the biggest hearts in the whole world."

He enveloped her in one of his spontaneous hugs. "I love you, Anna."

She hugged him back. "And I love you, Colm."

The bus pulled up and Colm got excited about dropping his money in the box. He enjoyed it so much, he put hers in, too. He took the seat right behind the driver. "Just in case someone's mean. I don't want ya to get in a fight."

"I promise I won't get in a fight, but I'll never let someone be mean to you. Someday, maybe you'll be by yourself, and if someone picks on you, you should—"

Colm didn't hear the part about someone picking on him. He honed immediately in on the other part. "D'ya think someday I can ride a bus by myself? I rode the school bus by myself once when Liam was sick, but it got me at the driveway and only ever went to school.

That was a real long time ago. But this bus stops lots of places and maybe I'd get lost."

"Well, we could practice until you were comfortable on the bus and you could try some little trips."

"Really, Anna?" He hugged her again.

"Really, Colm." She returned the hug and not for the first time felt rather blessed to spend her days working with such exceptional people. And Colm had moved beyond client. She hadn't lied. She was sure without any medical documentation that he had one of the biggest hearts ever.

"So, let's concentrate on when we get off the bus. We need to be downtown. On Main Street. By all the little stores—"

"And Macky's, right? We ain't gonna eat there, but we'll be by it. It's got a red-and-green thing over the door so that when it's rainin' you can stand there and not get wet. I always look for the red-and-green thing."

"Right. A red-and-green awning. So, you watch out the window and tell me when you think we're there."

"Okay, Anna, I'll watch and tell you."

He turned in his seat and faced out the window, staring as the streets flashed by.

Five minutes later, the bus finally left the side streets and pulled onto Main Street. "Hey, Anna, this is it. This is near Macky's, right? And Liam will meet us, right?"

"Right. When I called Liam and asked him if he'd like to have lunch with us, he said he'd meet us at the park."

"Let's go, let's go." He stood.

"No. Sit down until the bus stops."

Colm plopped back into the seat. "Oh, yeah, that was the rule on my old bus, too."

When the bus finally stopped at the small shelter on Main Street, Colm sprang to his feet like a jack-in-the-box whose lid had finally popped. "We're here, Anna. I got the bag with our lunch, so let's go find Liam."

She followed him off the bus. When he got on the sidewalk, he turned around and waved at the driver. "Bye, Mr. Bus Driver. I'll see you soon 'cause I'm gonna learn to ride a bus by myself. It's harder than a school bus."

The driver smiled.

Colm took Anna's hand. "Let's go eat, 'cause I'm starvin'. Busses is hard work."

They walked the couple of blocks to Wyndham Park, a tree-filled block in the center of town. There were benches, a few tables and some chess boards. In the summer, there was generally a contingent of people playing sports like Frisbee and football.

Anna and Colm found Liam waiting for them on a park bench. His hair was mussed. Anna couldn't decide if it was from the light spring breeze, or because Liam had run his fingers through it. His smile didn't quite reach his eyes. "You made it."

She wanted to ask what was wrong. A problem at work? She might not be able to follow his computer jargon, but she'd listen happily, if only to lessen that look of stress she saw in his expression.

Colm dropped Anna's hand and ran to his brother and hugged him. Anna saw Liam's expression soften as it always did, when he hugged Colm back. She wondered if he'd look as happy if they hugged…or if they did more than hug.

She very much wondered.

"…AND THE bus driver was so nice, Liam," Colm said as they sat on the picnic blanket

Anna had brought. "That bus driver, he's got a big heart, not like those kids who beat you up 'cause I'm dumb. They have small hearts, Anna says, and they probably hurt. But I think your face hurt when that Bartle kid hit you."

Liam glanced at Anna and could see that Colm had been telling her about the bus rides they used to take. "That was a long time ago, Colm. And you and I have both learned not to hit people."

"Yeah, but I still don't like that Bartle guy 'cause he hit you."

That statement summed up Colm in a nutshell.

He should have disliked Bartle because the guy had teased and picked on him. But no, Colm didn't like him because Bartle had hurt Liam.

Liam was thankful that Colm had never found out about most of his fights.

From the way Anna was looking at him, all caring and sympathetic, he hoped she never found out, either. He didn't want Anna feeling sorry for him. He wanted her…

He wanted her.

It was that plain and that complicated.

He wanted her to himself. And he felt a pang of guilt that he wanted time away from Colm.

Anna didn't seem to mind his brother tagging along. She told him as much, and for a while that had been fine with him because Colm provided him with a buffer.

The problem was, he didn't want a buffer any longer. There were a thousand reasons he shouldn't try to get any closer to Anna Chapel. He had a full plate what with running his software company and managing Colm.

Colm needed a lot of care and would always be his priority. And business had picked up to the extent that Liam was thinking it was time to hire more staff. He was putting it off because he liked his autonomy. He liked being in charge of everything. He didn't want to train and then supervise other people. His putting off hiring extra help was the reason he had such a raging headache today. Too much business for one man to handle.

He should have said no when Anna called and invited him to lunch today. He could have been partway to his next meeting in

Pittsburgh by now. Instead, he was lounging on a blanket in Wyndham Park with Anna and Colm.

He watched Anna unpacking the lunch with Colm, the two of them laughing at something he'd missed as he sat here woolgathering.

He knew what his next move was. Though he loved their outings and loved that she didn't mind going out with both him and Colm, he would arrange for Betty to stay with Colm one evening so that he and Anna could try another date.

And then…

He studied her as his brother talked. And couldn't stop himself from leaning over and whispering, "You look lovely today," in her ear. She didn't seem pleased by the compliment. As a matter of fact she seemed flustered. As if she wasn't used to it.

He'd be sure to compliment her more in the future. A woman should be accustomed to people saying nice things about her—to her.

"Liam, ya gotta taste your sandwich. I made it all by myself, but Anna told me how, so it tastes real good. I know 'cause I tasted it, but not the stuff I put on your sandwich.

That'd be gross to taste it then put it on someone's sandwich."

Liam ate his sandwich and praised Colm's emerging cooking abilities. And he noticed that Anna glowed over his comments as much as Colm did.

Anna liked being praised for actions more than for her looks. He recalled her once saying something similar.

Most women loved hearing they looked beautiful. And it was easy to say that about Anna. He'd seen her fuss with her hair, and that day on the beach, she'd muttered to herself as the wind whipped it out of its ponytail. But he loved it.

He loved that it was wild and natural. He still frequently felt the overwhelming urge to reach out and gently tug on a curl. And then he'd like to…

"Liam, you ain't eatin'," Colm complained.

He quit the image of Anna and concentrated on the lunch. "This is the best picnic I ever had."

"I know, it's my best, too," Colm said.

"My best three," Anna teased.

Colm looked puzzled.

Liam filled in, "My best four."

Anna grinned. "My best five."

"Oh, my best six," Colm said. "My best seven. My best eight."

"It's time to head back to the bus, Colm," Anna said, clearing up the picnic. "Aunt Betty will be waiting for you, and I have to see another client."

"Okay." He started to walk toward the bus stop. "My best eight. No, I did that. Nine. My best nine…"

"I think I started something I might regret," Anna admitted, as she picked up the bag.

Liam reached for it, to take it from her, and his hand brushed hers. "I'll see you two back to the bus stop."

They fell into step next to each other. Despite his height advantage, Anna didn't seem to have a problem keeping up. As she pulled slightly ahead of him, he watched her curls bounce and smiled. "Anna, could we try for that date again? Maybe tomorrow, if Betty can stay. Without Colm," he added, in case she'd missed his not-so-subtle invitation.

She turned back sharply enough to look at

him that her curls went flying in a dozen different directions. "Just the two of us?"

He nodded. "No Colm this time."

"Oh. I'd like that."

He was pretty sure he had a goofy grin on his face as he said, "Good." But try as he might, he couldn't seem to stop smiling. "Would you do me a favor?"

Anna nodded. "Sure."

"Wear that blue dress you had on for our first date."

She blushed again, and didn't respond.

"Will you?" he pressed.

"Yes."

"I'll call with specifics after I've talked to Aunt Betty."

"You know, Colm could probably stay on his own. We've been working on—"

"No," Liam said simply. There was no way he was leaving his brother on his own in the house. Granted, Colm was doing so much more than he'd ever imagined his brother could, but he wouldn't put Colm at risk like that. A fire. A stranger. No, Colm wasn't ready to stay alone, and Liam didn't think he ever would be. "No. I'll get someone to stay with him. If not Betty, then someone else."

"But Liam, he knows how to dial 911, he knows his address and we could leave someone's number. I've got some disposable cell phones from Sunrise. He can use one. My number's programmed into it. He's capable of being independent. Some of our clients will always be more dependent on others. And while Colm will always need help, he can function as an adult and—"

"Anna," Liam said softly. Nothing more than that because he didn't know what to say.

"Sunrise's goal is to help every client achieve their maximum potential, and Colm can do that and so much more."

Anna was pushing again, and while changes in the status quo still made Liam uncomfortable, he knew that she really believed that. She wanted what was best for Colm.

So did he.

He just wasn't sure what that meant.

He didn't have Anna's certainty.

But he didn't want to fight with her now, partly because he had no idea what he was fighting for or against anymore.

And partly because he very much wanted to kiss her.

He glanced at Colm, who was still counting quietly and heading for the street. Sure that the coast was clear, he leaned down and kissed Anna. He wasn't sure if it was to distract her from her argument or if it was just pure lust, either way, as his lips met hers, he was glad he'd done it.

Kissing Anna felt right.

If he wasn't very much aware that Colm was nearby, he could have gone on kissing her for some time. But he *was* aware, so he pulled back.

"Tomorrow. Friday. A solo date."

Anna beamed. "Yes, that might be a good idea."

ANNA DIDN'T HAVE to play the pick-the-clothing game before Friday's date because Liam had already requested the blue dress. She was happy to oblige, if only to keep herself from agonizing over choices again.

Aunt Betty had been more than happy to watch Colm. As a matter of fact, she'd been practically bursting with excitement over

Anna's date with Liam. "You two would be perfect together," the older woman had practically crooned.

Anna thought Betty was sweet, but she chafed at the notion that Colm had to have a babysitter. Chafed because she knew Colm could have managed a few hours on his own at home.

Liam had relaxed so much since that first meeting. He praised Colm's accomplishments and had let her have free rein. But there was still something—even when he wasn't voicing any complaints she could see that Colm's growing independence was a problem for him, and she wasn't sure why.

Maybe they'd discuss it tonight.

When the doorbell rang, she decided to cut to the chase and talk to him here, at her place. She answered the doorbell and started, "Liam, I..."

That's as far as she got. Despite her resolution, the second she saw Liam, her thoughts of a confrontation evaporated. She wasn't sure what it was, but every time she saw Liam her breath gave a little hitch. He could be the most exasperating man in the world, but still, he sort of made her turn to mush when he smiled at her.

And he was smiling at her now as he did a head-to-toe perusal of her outfit. "You wore it." His voice was husky.

"Yes," was all she could manage to say. She grabbed her purse from the hall table, turned and locked the door.

Liam reached out and took her hand in his. "I'm glad you wore it. You were such a good sport about our last attempt at a solo date. I wanted to take you somewhere nice. There's this winery in Ohio—Ferrante's. I thought we could drive there for dinner. It's a little bit of a drive?" The last sentence was more of a question than a statement.

"It's a beautiful night for a drive," she assured him. "It sounds lovely."

He paused at the passenger door to his car. "Before we officially start the date, I'd like to make a rule."

She chuckled. "A rule?"

"Yes. No shop talk. I won't talk computers, you won't talk Sunrise. We're simply two people on an official date. I want to know more about you, Anna." He gently ran his finger along her cheek. It made her breath hitch all over again.

He dropped his hand to his side and opened her car door for her. "That was a yes, you agree, right?"

"Yes," she assured him as she slid into her seat. He shut the door and she murmured, "I'd like to know more about you, too."

He walked around the car, got into the driver's seat and started the ignition.

It was a lovely May evening. The drive north on I-79 to I-90 was a quiet one. All their conversations to date had been about Colm. Now that it was only the two of them and Liam had announced his no-work-discussion policy, she wasn't sure what to say, and Liam wasn't making any opening conversational gambit.

They had another hour or so heading west on I-90 before they got to the restaurant, and Anna found herself wishing they'd stayed in Whedon and eaten at Macky's. Or even driven the short ride to Erie and eaten at one of the numerous Peach Street restaurants.

She felt as if she was suffocating in the silence. Liam had made up his rule because he wanted to know more about her, which was fine, because she wanted to know more about him, but if the silence persisted, the only thing she was going to know was how many mile markers there were between the two I-90 exits. She burst out, "Twenty Questions?"

Liam glanced over at her, then looked back at the road. "What?"

Anna was glad Liam couldn't watch her because she knew her suggestion was lame. "I can't think of anything else. We can take turns. Me first."

"Why do you get to go first?"

She could tell from his tone he was teasing, and she relaxed. "Because I thought of it, so I go first."

"Ooo-kay," he said slowly.

Anna decided to start with the basics. "Did you always live in Whedon?"

"Yes. You?"

Two words from him. That wasn't the most informative answer ever, but she'd take it. It was a start. "No. I was born in Erie and lived most of my childhood there. When my father died, Mom and I moved to Whedon. I was a junior in high school."

"I'm a couple of years older than you, so I'd have already graduated, which explains why I don't remember you from school. Whedon's small enough that I pretty much remember everyone in high school, at least vaguely. And I guarantee I wouldn't have forgotten you."

He took his eyes off the road, and there was enough heat in his glance that Anna felt flushed and flustered. She was saved from trying to come up with another question when he added, "That must have been hard on you, losing your dad then moving."

Anna remembered that year. It was probably the worst one of her life. "Mom couldn't keep up the payments on the house in Erie, and we moved into an apartment there. Then she got a job offer in Whedon, and it was easier to move than drive."

"Easier on her, not on you." He sounded annoyed on her behalf.

"I'd have never told Mom, but yeah, it was hard. After losing Dad, then the house I grew up in, we moved and I lost all my friends at Mercyhurst Prep and then started in the public school here. It was a bad time."

"I'm sorry."

"I'm not." Now that she thought about it, she wasn't. "The move might have been difficult at first, but it took me in a new direction. A good one. Along the way I realized that sometimes the hardest things are for the best. Ms. Marshal was my new homeroom teacher in Whedon. She ran the Special Ed department, and a few months into my first term, she asked if I'd mind helping one of her students. Julie was her name. I started volunteering a lot with Julie, then with Ms. Marshal's whole class. The time I spent there inspired me. It's why I took special education when I went to college. I thought I'd end up a Special Ed teacher like Ms. Marshal."

"Instead you went to work for Sunrise?"

"I tried the classroom, but there were always so many students that I felt as if I shortchanged all of them. I met Ceelie at different events here in town. Sunrise was a one-horse show at that point. She offered me a job. Technically, Ceelie's my boss, but with just the two of us, it's more of a partnership. Whedon's small enough that the two of us can handle most of its special needs residents.

Some of them require more than we can offer and travel into the Barber Center in Erie." She shrugged. "It's been three years and I still love it. I have a lot more autonomy. I can work one-on-one with the clients and tailor the lessons to their needs. I can work with adults, like Colm, or with younger students who are still in the school system. Some, like Colm, are higher functioning, and others are less so. But with all of them, I can help them go beyond their preconceived limits and—"

He cut her off. "I think we're straying into work. My turn for another question."

"No, you asked where I was from. That counted as a question, so it's my turn." And for a second she almost asked what his hobbies were. Another safe, inane question.

She'd spent most of her adult life on the safe side of the street and suddenly she didn't want to stay safe with Liam. With him, she wanted to try throwing caution to the wind, so she asked, "What are your dreams, Liam?"

Before he could answer, she clarified. "And I'm not talking about growing your business, or winning the lottery. I'm asking about for yourself. What do you dream about for you?"

He was quiet for a long while, then slowly answered, "I don't know if I've ever given it any thought. For years, it's been one step in front of the other. Finish high school—go to college. Finished college—go to work. Go to work—start my own business. Now the business is growing and I'm thinking about hiring help."

"And then there's your brother. There's Colm."

"Yes. My parents were in their forties when they had us, so I knew eventually I'd get Colm. Only I didn't think it would be so soon."

"They asked if you'd be his guardian?"

"No, they never asked. All of us always knew I would be. When I worked, I knew I was working not only for me, but for him. I've never seemed to have time for dreams. There was too much going on. There still is."

Anna felt a stab of sympathy for Liam. She pictured a young boy fighting for Colm on the bus, all bruised and battered. That boy never dreamed. He'd shouldered his burdens and got on with it. "That's sort of sad, Liam. Everyone should have a dream."

This time he didn't glance at her, and she

very much wished he would. Maybe she'd have some clue what he was thinking.

He asked, "So what is your dream, Anna?"

"I don't have big, grand dreams. Only little ones. That's what most of mine are. For instance, the first day I came to your house, I had porch envy."

"Porch envy?" He laughed.

"Yes. I've always dreamed about having a porch. When we lived in Erie, we had a porch, but when we moved to the apartment, we didn't. And my condo barely has a front stoop. But someday, I'll buy a house and it will have a huge porch. It will be painted something pretty and bright. Green, maybe. Kelly green. There will be white wicker furniture with big fat cushions." She got caught up in describing her dream porch. "And plants hanging over the railings. Spider plants with their long fronds cascading down toward the ground. And maybe some flowering plants. In the morning, I'll go out with my coffee and the paper. I'll sit there in one of my white wicker chairs and watch the neighborhood wake up. As time goes on, I'll know which neighbors are early birds and which ones aren't. Those early birds will wave to me as they come out and get their own papers, or the ones who run in the mornings will wave as they jog past me on my porch. I'll become a fixture. The neighbors will come to expect me there."

Anna looked at his profile as he stared at the road. She could really study him. He had prominent bone structure. Instead of making him look hard, it made him look steady. He was someone who could be counted on.

"And at night, I'll be coming home," she continued. "Not back to an apartment or condo, but to a home. And maybe after dinner, I'll find myself sitting on my porch, in my white wicker chair, and find someone sitting next to me."

"You've given this a lot of thought," Liam said.

"Maybe. Big front porches seem to connect a house to the neighborhood. I like that. I like porches."

"And you like little dreams like that."

"Yes."

He glanced at her again. There was something in his expression that said he was puzzled and she gave a nervous laugh. "I know. It sounds stupid."

He turned and looked back at the road, and said, "No, not stupid at all."

CHAPTER FIVE

LIAM FINALLY bit the bullet and quietly put out the word among some of his contacts that he was looking to hire someone to take some of the workload off his shoulders. He'd thought about what Anna had said about Sunrise being a one-horse show until Ceelie had hired her, and now they worked as partners. That's what he needed. Someone to pick up the slack.

His buddy Rob, who worked for the State Police's Internet Crime Division, had reminded him about their buddy, Benjamin Paul. Luckily, he'd spotted Ben at the coffee shop the following Friday. When he explained his predicament and showed Ben a mock problem, something lit up the man's eyes that had nothing to do with their startling blue color. Ben studied the problem intently, then said, "The access control list in the router is blocking the vpn. You need to create a permit rule for tcp traffic on port 1723. That will enable PPTP tunnels to be created through your router."

At those words, Liam knew he'd found his man.

"You're hired," he said on the spot.

They talked salaries and benefits.

Benjamin Paul was the perfect person for the job, but Liam felt a stir of unease. He knew the business was making enough money to support hiring an employee. Security for computer systems was a growing lucrative market. But he liked running everything himself. He liked the autonomy. His feelings were jumbled.

Nervous at the thought of turning over some of the control.

Happy the company was doing well enough to warrant this step.

Lucky he'd found someone as knowledgeable as Ben.

And thrilled that he'd have more time with Anna.

"So, there's no office?" Ben asked.

"For now, I work from my place. You can

work from home. I'll get you started. But Franklin Systems Security's next step will probably have to be obtaining a physical office space."

"I don't mind working from home. And from what you've said, most of your clients prefer you coming to their businesses, rather than them coming to your office, right?"

"Right."

The waitress came over, a pot of coffee in hand. "Refills?"

"No, I'm fine," Liam said.

"You can warm mine up, sweetheart." Ben flashed her a smile.

Liam watched as the waitress's face lit up. She poured the splash of coffee into his cup and said, "You holler if you need anything. Anything at all."

She sauntered away, a little extra swing in her hips. One that had never been there when she served Liam.

He turned to gauge Ben's reaction, but when the woman was out of Ben's line of sight, he was back to all-business mode. "If most of your meetings—our meetings—are at the clients' businesses, why add to your expenses now by looking for an office? Working from home makes fiscal sense. And most of what we do can be done right over the Net. Me in my house, you in yours."

"Ben, I like your way of thinking."

"Hey, it's selfish on my part. Beau's at home and he's used to me being there."

"A son?" Liam asked.

Ben shook his head. "No, a dog. A hundred-and-seventy-pound Old English mastiff. He thinks he's people, though."

"A hundred and seventy pounds?" Liam let out a low whistle. "Now, that's a dog."

"Yeah. I didn't want a frou-frou tiny dog." Ben chuckled.

"So, basically, you don't do things halfway," Liam said. That was a quality which was going to be very beneficial to Franklin Systems Security.

"All or nothing, that's my motto," Ben assured him. "You and Franklin Systems Security can count on that."

"Is Beau going to make travel difficult? That's one of the reasons I need help with the company, there's been more travel. I can't do it all. I have obligations at home, too."

"A dog?" Ben asked.

"No, a brother."

He expected Ben to ask for clarification, but instead he said, "No, travel won't be difficult. I've got a dog-sitter I use." Ben shut his laptop and asked, "So we've covered everything except when I start."

They talked another hour about specifics. Ben was a fast study.

As Ben left the meeting, Liam realized that if they split up the travel fifty-fifty, it was going to mean he'd have even more time with Anna.

Liam wasn't sure why Anna was one of the first things he thought about as he weighed the pros and cons, but he didn't want to analyze it. He wanted to share his news with her. He glanced at his watch. Two forty-five.

He knew she had a session with Colm today at three. If he went right home, he could catch her and invite her to dinner. A celebration.

The thought amused him as he sped home from the coffee shop. As he got out of the car, he could hear Colm's voice from the backyard, so rather than heading into the house, he walked around it. Anna and Colm were both laboring over something on the picnic table under the maple tree. Anna hadn't put her hair in a ponytail today, so as she leaned over to look at whatever they were doing, her curls tumbled forward.

Liam stood at the corner of the house watching the two of them.

"…and that's a bird on the rainbow." Colm pointed to something on the table. Liam assumed it was a picture.

Liam must have moved or made some noise because Colm's attention switched from the table to Liam. "Hey, Liam." He went from stationary to running in the blink of an eye and hurled himself at Liam, enveloping him in a huge hug. "Aunt Betty wants to know if I can have a sleepover at her house. We got a new movie, and we're gonna make popcorn and stay up really late—maybe all night, if she don't fall asleep. And Mr. Gerry says he'll take me fishin' tomorrow, if that's okay. I won't fall in or anythin'."

Liam nodded. "That's fine."

"I'll go tell her." He bolted toward the house.

"You look happy," Anna said, as she

gathered up the paper and paints that were spread across the picnic table.

"I have a new employee. Actually Franklin Systems Security does. He's starting tomorrow."

"Congratulations. That should make things easier on you."

"Do you want to celebrate with me tonight? I thought the three of us could go out, but since Colm is going to Betty's, it would be just us." He pulled her into his arms and kissed her. "I'll buy you dinner. We could drive to Erie."

"Or," Anna said.

"Or what?"

"Or we could order in. Colm was my last appointment for the day, so I'm all yours."

Liam was sure Anna hadn't meant the words the way they sounded, but his body didn't know that. It had tightened in a most uncomfortable manner. He forced himself to ignore how much he wished Anna had meant the words exactly the way that they'd sounded and concentrated on dinner. Ordering in.

"We could order Chinese, if you like Chinese food," Anna added.

"Since when did Whedon get a Chinese restaurant?" Liam asked.

"We didn't. Colm and I went to Macky's the other day for burgers, and they've got a new Chinese menu."

"You're sure you're willing to try Chinese from a burger joint?"

Anna laughed. "Sometimes, you've got to throw caution to the wind." She kissed him. It was the smallest of pecks on the cheek. "Has Colm ever packed for an overnight by himself?"

"No." Before Anna, Colm hadn't done much by himself.

Before Anna.

He seemed to think that a lot.

"Then I'd better go supervise." She kissed him again. "Congrats on your new employee."

Liam trailed after her and watched as she hustled Colm upstairs to pack.

"So, did you hire this one?" Aunt Betty asked as she tidied around the kitchen.

"Yes." And Liam was forgetting his anxiety about hiring someone. He was thinking about how much more time he'd get to be at home. With Colm.

With Anna.

"Good," Aunt Betty said, wiping her wet hands on a towel. "After you didn't even consider the last three—"

"They were nowhere near qualified."

"—I figured you would never let go of the reins totally and get the help you need." Without waiting for him to respond, she said, "Colm mentioned you agreed to let him come spend a night at our place."

"Yes. That is if you're sure."

"Gerry will love having someone to fish with," she said. "He used to take our nieces and nephews, but they've long since gotten too busy for him. I don't know why I didn't think of inviting Colm before."

"Maybe because you assumed Colm wouldn't be able to. Just like I assumed he couldn't do so many things he does quite readily now." Because of Anna, he thought again.

"Anna's made a difference," she said, as if she'd read his mind.

"Yes." And not only with his brother.

"You be careful, Liam. I know you don't appreciate hearing someone else's opinion, but that girl is special. She's not someone you date for a while, then dump. I don't think she does things halfhearted. If she starts, she's all in. She's not here to be used."

The accusation hurt. "I don't use women, Betty."

"You do. Not in a mean way, but you and I know that you're not going to get serious with them, and they all end up serious about you. And that hurts. I don't want that for Anna."

"I don't either." He did date now and then, but Colm had made things difficult. Even before his parents died, Colm had been his test—watching how the women he dated reacted to Colm. He always made it clear that Colm came first. That didn't tend to sit well, and—

"Be careful," Betty continued. "I fear you're playing with fire and you don't even know it. And I'm not worried that you're the one going to get burned. I'm worried about Anna."

"I don't know what to say." He genuinely cared for Anna and she understood and accepted Colm in a way no other woman ever had. She really liked Colm for himself.

She saw how special he really was. "Aunt Betty, I—"

"Don't say anything, just be careful of that girl. I like her. She's good people."

After Betty left, taking Colm with her, her warning continued to bother him. He wasn't sure why. He listened as Anna ordered more food than the two of them could ever eat from Macky's.

"Why don't we go out and sit on the front porch and wait," Anna said.

Thankful for something to do, Liam agreed. "Want something to drink first?"

"I think Aunt Betty made lemonade." Anna didn't wait for him to get it, she walked into the kitchen and poured them each a glass. She didn't ask where the glasses were. She navigated his kitchen with the same efficiency that Betty did.

They sat on the porch holding their lemonades. A jogger went by, Anna smiled and waved.

She sighed happily. "I do love your porch."

"Porch envy, right?" He laughed. Anna's statement about dreaming little things stuck with him. What made him happy?

Anna.

At this moment, sitting with her on his porch with a lemonade in his hand, he was very happy.

What were his dreams? That he hadn't figured out yet.

Patrick from next door got dropped off. He spotted them as he wheeled his walker up his driveway. "Hey, Li, Anna. Enjoy the night. It's a beauty, all right."

Anna waved and called back, "Yes it is. A beautiful evening. Enjoy." She sat back and gave another contented sigh. "I really like your neighbors. Patrick's a character. He caught me leaving one afternoon and told me that my name meant gracious. He then proceeded to tell me that potatoes Anna is a French potato dish. By the time he was done, I knew more about the origins of my name than anyone should."

"I think I must have inspired that particular conversation. He'd been filling me in on my name as well." He remembered that conversation. Warrior? He didn't feel like a warrior. As he'd told Anna, he'd never really had any dreams…he'd taken the next step, whatever it was. There'd been no fighting for any of it, simply one step after the next.

"Don't leave me in suspense," Anna said. "Your name means?"

"Liam means warrior, Colm means dove."

She smiled and nodded in agreement. "Do you think your mom knew what they meant when she named you?"

"No. We were named after her dad and his brother. They came over from Ireland together and bought a farm in Crawford County. Great-Uncle Colm never married. He had a small shanty behind the big house and worked next to my grandfather his entire adult life. Mom loved him best, I think. He was never too busy to tell her a story. She told them to me and Colm when we were little."

"I like names that mean something."

"And you? Why'd your parents name you Anna?"

She took a long sip of her lemonade before saying, "My dad was Antonio. Antonio Chapel. My mom had a lot of complications with her pregnancy, and for a while, they didn't think either of us would make it. My father was terrified. He swore there would be no more babies. My mother fought, but he wouldn't listen. So, she named me after him. It's really Antonia, but I was always Anna. I like that he left me that piece of himself."

A young couple pushing a stroller walked by. Anna called out a merry, "Hi," and they both waved.

"I love this."

He recognized that she was changing the subject, and he got that. She'd shared something deeply personal and needed some space from it, so he simply said, "What do you love?"

"I know I might have mentioned it before," she laughed a small tinkling sound. "But sitting on the porch and watching the world go by. I love it." She gave another happy sound that was akin to a sigh, but it was a signal of absolute pleasure.

Such a little thing to make someone so happy. "Watching the world go by makes you happy." It wasn't a question. He didn't need to ask because he knew that it did.

"I have friends who are always working toward that next big thing that will make them happy. A promotion. An expensive new car. A beach house. Flying to some exotic destination for vacation. But to be honest, driving a new car doesn't matter to me. Living in a ritzy house or going on expensive vacations don't either."

"Jewels?" he teased.

She held up her totally unadorned hands. "Nope."

"But things like front porches do." Again, a statement. He was understanding her more and more.

She nodded again. "Sunsets on Presque Isle. Seagulls, too."

Just to get a rise out of her, he said, "Seagulls are flying rats."

"Hey." He saw when it registered that he was teasing and she grinned.

"They're not flying rats. They're beautiful. I love the sound of their cries. I can't imagine living in a section of the country where there were no seagulls."

"They eat anything. Definitely rats."

"You and Colm eat anything, too, but hey, I don't hold that against you," she joked. And then laughed at herself.

Liam couldn't help but join in.

"So front porches and other little things?"

At that moment, Liam totally understood because while sitting on the porch with Anna, he was happy. It might seem like nothing, but to him it was a big thing.

She turned and studied him. Curls bounced around her shoulders. And this once, Liam didn't even try to resist. He reached out and wound one curl around his finger.

Anna froze.

"Speaking of little things, your hair has fascinated me since that first day."

"It's not a little thing. It's a huge animal nest. I can't control it. I tried cutting it short, but that was even worse. At least some weight settles it a bit."

"I'm glad you let it grow out again."

"I…"

A beat-up station wagon pulled into the driveway and a teenaged boy got out with a bag in hand. "You guys order Chinese?"

Liam dropped Anna's curl and reached for his wallet. He turned back to Anna on the porch. "We could eat out here, if you want to watch the world go by some more."

"No, I've had enough of the world for now. I'd like to spend some time with you—only you and me." She took the bag in one hand, and his hand in her other and led him inside. Anna closed the door and as they stood in the hallway, she kissed him. "I don't want any promises of tomorrow, Liam. I'm not looking for an ever-after. I know that in this one moment, I want you. And I think you want me."

Of all the understatements in the world, this was the biggest. Liam took the bag of take-out from her, set it on the pile of mail and led her up the stairs.

Had she asked for forever, he would have walked away because he knew he didn't have forever to promise anyone but Colm. Taking care of his brother, that was his forever. But she'd only asked for now…this moment. And that he could give her.

A moment he could give himself.

Maybe that made him selfish, but for once he was going to do something for himself.

Just this one moment for himself and Anna.

THE NEXT MORNING, Anna woke up in Liam's bed at six feeling confused.

She'd spent the night.

That was something she'd never done

before and she wasn't sure of the protocol. Was she supposed to stay here until Liam woke up? Should she gather her things, tiptoe out and make an escape? Should she go downstairs and make coffee for them both?

She'd told Liam last night that she liked the little things, like sitting on a front porch in the evening.

Well, that's how she liked her relationships, too. Little. Nothing big and overwhelming. A relationship worked until…well, until it didn't. She didn't want anything that could make her lose herself like her mother did with men, time after time. And part of that not losing herself meant never spending a night at someone else's house.

Until last night.

She glanced at the man sleeping next to her. His brown hair was mussed and he seemed stress-free, which made him look younger. Her hand itched to reach out and brush his hair back from his face. But she didn't.

She couldn't lie here all day watching Liam Franklin sleeping, so she rolled slowly away and slipped out of bed. She scanned the floor in search of clothing. She found panties right next to the bed, her jeans were on a chair, and her bra was hanging from the lamp. She didn't see her shirt and wondered if it was on Liam's side of the bed, or in the hall. She put on what she'd found and decided to go look for her shirt.

"Are you leaving?" Liam asked lazily from the bed.

Anna stopped in her tracks, feeling very exposed without her shirt on. She knew it was ridiculous, that Liam had seen her in less than this last night, but knowing and feeling are two different things. "I don't want Aunt Betty and Colm to come back and find me here in the same clothes I wore yesterday."

"I wish you didn't have to go."

"But we both know I do. We don't want either of them to have unrealistic expectations."

"About that…"

She leaned over and kissed him. "I don't have any unrealistic expectations either, Liam. This was what it was. Two people. One night. I've always thought relationships will run their course. Right now, this is good. It feels right. But when it stops feeling right, then it stops. No regrets. No recriminations. It will simply be over."

"I don't want to lead you on. I have Colm. That means I can never put a relationship first. Most women don't like that." He paused and then added, "Aunt Betty warned me about hurting you."

She kissed him again and realized she wanted nothing more than to pull off what clothes she had on and climb into bed with him. But she'd meant it, she didn't want Colm walking in and catching them. She felt like a teenager sneaking around.

"Aunt Betty doesn't need to worry. I'm a big girl and I came to your room last night knowing exactly what I was getting into. You're not leading me on. Remember last night on the porch when I said I like little things?"

Liam started choking. After a moment he managed to gasp, "I hope you're not about to tell me that I'm being added to your little-thing list."

Even after spending a night with him, she knew she was blushing. "No. No. What I meant was, I'm not looking for an epic ever-after love story. I'm looking for something that makes me happy now. When it no longer makes me happy, then it's over."

"And right now?"

"You make me very happy." She glanced at her watch. "But I'm still leaving before anyone else catches us."

He laughed. "You'll be back later to work with Colm?"

"Yes, later."

She found her shirt in the hall, around the corner from Liam's bedroom. Her socks were on the stairs. She wasn't going to puzzle about why her socks had been the first thing she took off. Last night it must have made sense to her, but this morning it struck her as odd.

Dressed, she was ready to go. But first she had to get to her car, which had been parked in the driveway all night. That meant everyone in the neighborhood knew she'd spent the night. Anna felt uncomfortable at the thought. Again, she knew it was ridiculous. She was an adult and had every right to sleep over if she wanted. But she still hoped no one would see her as she made her way to her car.

She had her hand on the handle, when

Patrick Yu called her name and waved. He was standing on his front porch, his newspaper in hand. "Good morning, Anna."

She managed a small wave of her own. "Morning, Patrick."

She opened her car door and slipped in. All she wanted to do was go home and grab a shower.

She didn't want to speculate on why she felt so guilty about leaving like this.

The walk of shame. She'd read articles on that. Women who left a date the next morning in the same clothes they'd started their date in.

Mixing business with personal matters wasn't her normal modus operandi, but rather than weigh and measure her decision, she decided to revel in her happiness. Because right now she was very, very happy.

CHAPTER SIX

TWO WEEKS LATER, Anna and Colm stood in the parking lot of Keller's Market. She found it hard to believe it was already mid-June and that she'd been working with Colm for two months. Her stomach was a mass of butterflies, which was always the case when her clients began traveling on their own.

She reassured herself that she'd prepared Colm as much as anyone could. They'd ridden the bus frequently, and for the last two weeks they'd done the shopping for the house, taking the bus to and from Keller's. Colm knew the route, and knew that if he got stuck he could ask the bus driver.

She could go over what they'd done a dozen more times, and she knew she'd still be nervous. More nervous than she usually was because Colm had long since stopped being just a client.

He was a friend. A kindred spirit. Someone she truly enjoyed being with, respected, learned from, in fact. He was special, and she knew it.

She shouldn't have allowed it to happen, but now there was nothing she could do about it. It was done. She couldn't push him out of her heart any more than she could push Liam away.

There was something rather irresistible about the Franklin brothers.

"Now, you have your cell phone?" she asked.

Colm patted his left jeans pocket. "Check."

"And your fare?"

This time he patted his right pocket. "Yep."

"And you remember what you're going to do?"

"I ride until I get to Main Street, where we got off for the picnic, then I switch and get on the bus to home."

"And when you get off that bus?"

"I gotta walk for two blocks and cross the brick house's street."

"Right. And you remember your address?"

He repeated it back to her, then continued,

"And I don't talk to strangers. I don't get off the bus with nobody nowhere but at my stop."

"Right."

"'Cause most people are nice," he continued, "but sometimes there are bad ones and nobody can tell from the outside if someone's nice or bad. It's the inside that matters. If they got big hearts like me, or little hearts like that guy Bartle who beat up Liam."

Anna didn't think Liam realized how badly that incident so many years ago had bothered Colm. Every time they rode a bus, he was reminded of it and mentioned it. And whenever Colm said the name *Bartle* it sounded like a swear word, which seemed so incongruous with Colm's easygoing way.

"Right, you can't tell big hearts from the way someone looks on the outside," she agreed.

Colm reached out and hugged her. "Don't worry, Anna. You taught me good. I'm gonna ride this bus, 'cause if I can learn to navible—" he paused.

"Navigate," she supplied.

He nodded his head vigorously. "Yeah, navigate, then I can do all sort of things, like get a job, right?"

She'd looked around for the perfect position for Colm and had talked to Zac Keller at Keller's Market a few weeks ago about the possibility. Zac was a nice guy who had made the family-owned grocery store a part of the community in a number of ways. He'd been enthusiastic at the idea of hiring one of Sunrise's clients. Anna thought Colm would be a good match for Keller's. He could work at tasks that were well within his abilities, and he'd have a chance to interact with people. That's why they were trying the first solo trip from this parking lot.

"Right. When you can ride the bus all by yourself, then we'll think about jobs after we talk to Liam."

Colm's smile evaporated, replaced by a worried look. "Will Liam let me?"

She wanted to assure him that Liam would. She thought that Liam would. But they'd yet to talk about it. They'd been getting along so well lately, she'd been hesitant to rock the boat. She was at home with this new Liam— her lover—and she didn't want to risk taking a step backward and reawakening the man who'd first come to Sunrise.

That made her a coward.

Looking at Colm getting ready to make this huge move of independence, she felt her lack of courage. When they all celebrated Colm's success tonight, she'd bite the bullet and bring up the idea of Colm and a job.

The Whedon city bus pulled into the grocery-store parking lot.

"Okay, here I go, Anna." Colm was practically radiating his excitement.

The butterflies in her stomach kicked up a notch. "Now, remember everything we've gone over, Colm. I'll be waiting at your house. If there's any trouble, you get on your cell phone—"

"And call you. I know, Anna."

The bus pulled up at the bench and the door swung open. Colm climbed the stairs, reached in his pocket, pulled out his money and dropped it in the box as if he'd been doing it all his life, not merely the last few weeks. Then he chose the first available seat and waved at her through the glass as the bus pulled away.

Anna stood there a few minutes, watching the bus disappear down the street, then she strode to her car, in a hurry to get back to Liam's. She didn't want to take any chances and have Colm arrive home before she could get there.

She was surprised to see Liam's car in the driveway as she pulled in behind him. She thought he'd said he had meetings today.

She shut her car door as he came out onto the porch. He smiled when he spotted her. It was a slow, easy smile that made her heart accelerate.

His smile dimmed a notch as he looked at the car, and then back at her. "Where's Colm?"

Anna felt a surge of nervousness. "He should be here in a bit. He's taking the bus."

"By himself?" The dimming of his smile progressed to an out-and-out frown.

She forced a smile and nodded. "Yes. We've been practicing for weeks. He knows what to do." She tried to offer up the sentence as if Colm riding the bus by himself was the most natural thing in the world.

Liam wasn't buying it. "How do you practice dealing with jerks? There's no one to stand up for him if someone hassles him. And what if he gets lost?"

In her mind's eye, she'd seen Colm announcing his achievement to Liam and Liam glowing with pride on his brother's behalf. Not this anger. That wasn't what she'd imagined. She didn't know what to do with it. She hadn't dealt with this Liam in a long time. She'd expected resistance at the idea of Colm working, but not about this. Or if she was honest, maybe she had secretly feared just this and that's why she wanted to present it as a done deal. "I—"

"I trusted you, Anna."

"Liam, take a breath. This was all outlined in that original paperwork I gave you. We have discussed it a bit. Sunrise's goals, my goals for Colm are to help him be as independent as possible. There's a list of criteria a client needs to meet to move on to the next step. Colm met that criteria for a solo bus ride. He can do this. This is why I'm here, to help him do—"

"You are not here to put him in danger."

"I'm here to help him learn as much as he can. You only need to give him a chance." She wanted to ask him to give her a chance, but she didn't. This was about Colm. It had to be about Colm.

The fact that she was dating Liam fuzzied the margins, and not for the first time, she doubted her wisdom in dating a client's guardian.

She'd thought she could separate her affection for Liam and her job mentoring Colm, but now she wasn't so sure. With the family of another client, she probably would have given them a heads-up that a next step was coming. But because she was dating Liam, she'd tried not to talk too much about what she was doing with Colm, since there was no way to tell sometimes if Liam was ready for a new level of Colm's independence.

The fact was, she didn't want to fight with Liam, period. That made her naive and a coward.

"Let's sit down," she said, gesturing to the porch.

Liam scowled, then sat down in one of the lawn chairs.

Anna took the other one. She knew she owed Liam an apology and an explanation. "While we're waiting, I want to explain—"

"I don't want explanations and excuses, and I don't want to make small talk, Anna. I want to wait for my brother."

Anna didn't know what to say to him, so she simply replied, "Fine."

They sat silently, waiting.

Anna checked her watch repeatedly. She should have timed exactly how long the trip should take Colm. Whedon wasn't that big and she was pretty sure he should have been here by now.

She wouldn't let Liam's worry infect her. Colm would be here soon, or he'd call.

"Where is he?" Liam burst out.

She repeated what she'd been thinking. "He'll be here. He's perfectly safe, Liam. This is Whedon. Not some big city. It's not even a small city like Erie. It's a blink-twice-and-miss-it sort of town with one traffic light that the mayor installed mainly for show. Colm's fine. We've practiced and he has a cell phone—"

"I'm going to call him," he pulled out his cell phone. "What's the number?"

"No," she said.

"No? You're seriously not going to give me the number?"

She couldn't decide if the look he shot her was anger or surprise. He didn't seem exactly sure, either.

Anna believed it was a mixture of both.

He said, "What if something's happened to him? You can't tell me no, Anna. So we're seeing each other, it doesn't give you any right over my brother. Colm is ultimately my responsibility."

"Liam, it's killing me, too. But Colm needs to do this on his own. If you insist, I'll give you the number, but I think calling this soon would be a mistake on our parts. Colm needs to learn to trust himself. And that includes making mistakes and correcting them. He knows he's supposed to call me if he has a problem."

Liam glanced at his watch. "It's been too long. He must have had a problem."

"Maybe. Probably. But don't go rushing in. He's so excited about this. And he's an adult, Liam. For years, no one seemed to remember that. Maybe he functions at a different level than most people, but he needs to do things on his own. That includes making mistakes. I'm not suggesting he learn to drive. I don't think that's a possibility. But he can learn the bus system. He can learn to navigate Whedon. He can learn so much, do so much, Liam. You have to give him a chance." Anna knew what she was really asking—that he trust she was a competent teacher who knew what she was doing.

At least she hoped she knew what she was doing.

She resisted the urge to look at her watch.

"Colm can and should learn." Liam's voice was tight, as if he were really working at remaining composed. He was clenching the arms of the lawn chair so tightly that his knuckles were taking on a white tinge. "Things like making his bed or cooking. Those are safe steps toward independence. Maybe my family was wrong all these years and did too much for him, sheltered him too much. But you don't know what it was like when he was in school. The kids were—"

She looked at him, so angry with her, so frustrated. Hurting for the cruelty of kids so many years ago. "Liam, Colm can do this. And he needs to do it on his own. If he makes a mistake, he needs to be the one to fix it. This isn't school. Okay, he has some limitations, but all of us do, of one kind or another. Trust him."

She thought he was going to insist she give

him the number, and she'd have to. But he merely gave a curt nod of his head. "But if he's not here in the next twenty minutes, I'm calling him."

They went back to their silent waiting.

Anna felt as if a giant clock was ticking.

Where was Colm? She wouldn't admit it to Liam, but she wanted to call him, as well. But she didn't. He needed to figure this out.

It wasn't as if she'd put him on a bus in New York City.

This was Whedon.

There were only a few options with the bus routes. But they could be long routes, so if he stayed on past his stop and if he didn't realize right away, that would explain the length of time it was taking.

Liam checked his watch. "Anna."

"A few more minutes, Liam." As if on cue, her cell phone rang and she pulled it from her pocket. "Hello?"

"Anna, it's me, Colm. I goofed up, Anna. I goofed up real bad."

He didn't sound scared. He sounded mad. Mad that he'd made some mistake. "Hey, everyone makes mistake. If you spill it…"

"Clean it up." She could almost hear his smile.

Liam was not smiling. He held his hand out, indicating she should let him talk. She shook her head and shifted as far from him as she could get and still be in her chair.

"So, where are you, Colm?"

"I don't know. I got off the bus, but this ain't the right brick house. Maybe I got on the wrong bus when I switched. Maybe I'm lost. Maybe—"

She interrupted him, wanting to stop him before he panicked. "Are you still at the bus stop?"

"Yeah."

"So, what do you think you should do?"

He was quiet a long minute, and finally said, "I could wait here and ask the next bus driver?"

"Right. Do you remember your address?"

He repeated it.

"Right. So, if you tell the next bus driver your address…?"

"He can tell me what bus. He can help me, 'cause bus drivers are nice. That's why I sit in the front seat, 'cause bus drivers don't let no one pick on you."

"Bus drivers are nice."

"Okay, I'll wait right here, Anna. This is just a little mess, right?"

"It's only a little mess."

"Yep," he said, all traces of his anger at himself gone. "If you make a mistake, you gotta clean it up. If you spill the milk, you wipe it up."

"No problem, Colm. This is a little mess."

"Okay, Anna. I'm gonna wait right here for the next bus. And I ain't gonna go anywhere else or talk to strangers or nothin'. I messed up, so now I'll clean it up. I'll fix it."

"I know you will, Colm."

"And it's okay to ask the bus driver for help, right?" Uncertainty was back in his voice.

"Right. Everyone needs help once in a while. Remember the other day when Liam couldn't find his phone?"

"And I found it for him, 'cause he needed my help. Everyone needs help. 'Specially when the bus gets all goofy." He paused a split second and asked, "You still waitin'?"

"Yes. I'm not going anywhere until you're home. I'm sitting here on the porch watching for you."

"I knew that, Anna. You'll always wait for me," he said with utter confidence. "Okay, I'll see ya soon."

"See you soon, Colm."

"Hey, Anna," he shouted before she could hang up. "I love you."

A huge lump of emotion formed instantly in her throat. "I love you, too, Colm."

He hung up.

"So?" Liam said. Not really said. He sort of snarled it.

"So. He stayed on the bus too long and got off at the wrong location. But he's still at the bus stop and is waiting for the next one, then asking for help."

"We could go get him."

"We could, but what we should do is wait here. He wasn't scared, Liam," she said in an effort to reassure him. "He was upset at himself for messing up. You need to assure him that everyone makes mistakes and it's okay. You fix them yourself, or you ask for help if you need it. Either way, you fix it."

Liam turned without saying another word and paced the length of the porch—back and forth, back and forth. He didn't say a word for more than twenty minutes. Maybe it was longer. Anna didn't want to have him see her checking the time, so she sat in the chair staring out at the street, hoping that Colm would come around the corner.

Finally, Liam paused in front of Anna. "If anything happens to him, I'm going to blame you."

If anything happened to Colm, she'd blame herself because it would mean she hadn't done a good enough job of teaching him what he needed to know. "Liam, he's fine. He's practiced and has a phone. He knows—"

"We were fine. Colm and I—we were fine. Content. I came to you to find a sitter for when Betty couldn't help, and instead, I get you in here pushing and prodding. Meddling in our lives. And now you've put my brother in danger. I'm not only talking about the fact he could get lost or end up in the wrong part of town and get hurt, I'm talking about the people out there who could hurt him. Do you know what it's like to have people tease him? Call him names? At least when I'm with him, I can take care of him. But you've sent him out there on his own. Who's going to take care of him?"

"You think that's what I want? People hurting him? Colm can take care of himself. Well, he's learning to. And in case you didn't know it, Colm's never mentioned times people hurt his feelings. You know what's bothered him the most? That time you fought with Bartle over him. All these years, he's remembered that and it's bothered him, because you got hurt."

"I didn't know," Liam admitted.

Anna reached out and put her hand lightly on top of his. "I know you didn't. But—"

Liam suddenly pulled his hand out of her grasp. "I think we should call this all off. I'll find my own babysitter for Colm when I have to travel and Betty can't be here. But with my new hire, I shouldn't be gone as much. Now that I've hired Ben, I won't really need you at all."

Anna tried to ignore how much his words hurt. "Just like that? You're going to call it off? Despite the progress Colm's made?"

"Colm and I don't need you. Everything was fine before you came."

"Everything wasn't fine. You were treating Colm like a child, but he's not a child. He's a grown man who has hopes and dreams. He's got so much potential, and you want to ignore that?"

"I want my brother to be safe."

Anna wanted to reach out and touch him again, but she didn't. "Liam, you can't bubble-wrap your brother. What if something happens to you? What then? Where does Colm go from there?"

"There's no reason to think—"

She interrupted him. "There's every reason to think. Look at what happened to your parents. They didn't think they'd be in an accident. But they'd made arrangements. They left you to take care of Colm. But if you die? If something happens and you're physically not able to care for him, what then, Liam? What about Colm then?"

"I don't know, but I'll figure it out."

"Colm can learn to care for himself. He can have a job—"

"What kind of job can Colm hold down? He can read, but at barely a first-grade level. He can count, but not much more than twenty, at least not consistently. What, Anna? What kind of job can my brother do?"

"I already have an interview for him at Keller's Market. That's part of *my* job, Liam. I'd go in with him for the first few weeks and help him adjust. He can stock shelves and clean and—"

"When were you going to tell me about this?"

"Tonight. After he'd shown he could ride the bus by himself. I wanted to give you an example of how much Colm can do—"

"Go ahead and say it."

"Say what?" she asked.

"All the things that Colm can do that I've kept him from trying. You wanted to ease me into it, because somehow you think you know what Colm needs better than I do."

"I wasn't going to say that, Liam, we've had this conversation before. You're a good brother. After you assumed responsibility for Colm, you kept him safe and helped him adjust. You—"

"Don't patronize me, Anna. I don't need you trying to soothe me and jolly me into realizing you're right."

"That's not what I'm doing. I just—"

"Anna, Liam, I made it," Colm cried

from the sidewalk. "I did it, Anna. I did it by myself."

They both hurried off the porch and down the stairs to meet Colm.

"I knew you could do it, Colm." Anna caught Liam's flinch as she said the words and didn't know what to do. She'd hurt him...again.

"Did you hear that, Liam? I can ride the bus by myself. The bus driver was so nice. I said I got a little lost, but Anna says everybody needs help, right, Anna?"

"Yes, Colm." Anna was still watching Liam and wished she could find some way to help him as well. She wasn't sure why he was so resistant to Colm's growing independence. She ran into it sometimes with parents who felt guilty because of their child's problem. As if somehow it was their fault their child was born with obstacles to overcome and that by sheltering that child, they were paying penance. She understood that, and had helped parents get over their guilt.

Well, maybe *get over* was too optimistic a term. *Accept.* That was better. She'd helped parents learn to accept that sometimes things happen. Things that no one could control.

She understood that reaction in parents, but not in a brother, not with Liam.

"I did it, Liam. Did you hear? I rode a bus from the store all the way home by myself. I didn't need you to give me a ride."

"No, you didn't need me," Liam answered. Rather than sounding excited at not being needed, he sounded sad. "You did it on your own, bud."

"Well, me and that bus-driver guy who helped me." Colm was practically hopping with excitement. If Liam hadn't been here looking all stern and angry, Anna would have been tempted to teach Colm how to do a Snoopy Dance of Joy. But watching Liam, she didn't feel very joyful. She felt as if whatever they had was over. And, though she didn't count on relationships lasting forever, this one was ending too soon. Way too soon.

"So, now I can do stuff by myself, Liam. Anna can show me how to ride the bus to everywhere. Oh, oh. I can do the shopping for you now, 'cause I know how to get home from Keller's Market, right, Anna?"

"Right, Colm." She wondered if Liam had been serious when he'd for all intents and purposes fired her. His strained expression told her he'd been deadly serious.

Colm didn't seem the least bit aware of the anger radiating off Liam in waves. "And I bet if you made a list, I could buy the stuff, Liam. I can count money okay. I can do a lot of things by myself with help. Right, Anna?"

She glanced at Liam who wasn't meeting her eyes. "Right, Colm."

He was still angry at her. She didn't blame him. She should have prepared him and discussed the bus ride. Discussed Colm applying for a job.

Not wanting to rock a relationship boat wasn't a good excuse. Anna was good at rocking the boat at work, but not so good when it came to her personal life.

"Hey, Anna, let's go get dinner, 'kay? Right, Liam? Let's all go get some burgers. I like burgers. Hey, and I'll tell you where to turn, 'cause I got to learn how to get around so next time I don't make no mistakes on the bus."

"Colm, I'd love to go to dinner and celebrate with you, but I have other plans tonight." When his face fell, she quickly said, "But maybe tomorrow when I come over, we can go to the ice cream store?" She held her breath, waiting for Liam to tell her no, not to bother to come over, but he didn't.

And Colm, still not noticing his brother's silence, said, "Ice cream is good. Good idea, Anna. And we can take the bus. I'll show you how, Anna, 'cause I'm good at riding the bus now."

"I'll see you tomorrow, Colm." And softer she added, "Liam."

"I'll see you tomorrow, Anna," Liam said.

She breathed a sigh of relief. She wasn't fired. At least not yet.

ANNA HEADED to Ceelie's with a bottle of wine and wedge of brie in hand. Ceelie answered the door with a phone to her ear and a box of crackers tucked under her arm. "Yes... Uh-huh..."

Anna left her friend to her conversation, went into the kitchen and found the bottle opener and the wineglasses, then poured them each a glass. She was busy setting up the cheese when Ceelie joined her, no longer on the phone.

"Want the good news or the bad news?" Ceelie asked by way of a salutation.

"Your choice."

"The good news is, the new house got the variance from the zoning board."

Anna tried to muster up some enthusiasm and pasted a smile on her face. It felt brittle and fake, but it was the best she could do. "That isn't just good news, it's great news. Now, I'm almost afraid to ask about the bad news."

Ceelie took a sip of the wine. "The neighbors are in an uproar and protesting it. They have a petition and claim a group home in their neighborhood will lower their property values."

"Oh," was all Anna could think to say as the news sank in. "Did they know we aren't talking a large number of residents? There's only three?"

"I don't know what they know, but they're firmly against the idea."

"Oh," Anna said again. She took a fortifying swallow of her wine. "So now what?"

"We all have to appear before City Council. They'll get to present their case, we'll present ours, and Council will decide."

She felt sick to her stomach and she pushed the wineglass away. "This is going to be a day for the record books."

"What else happened?" Ceelie had that mom quality in her voice. The tone that said, tell-me-everything-and-I'll-try-to-make-it-better.

"Colm took his first solo excursion on a bus." This announcement about a client would normally be accompanied by a huge sense of elation. Not this time.

Ceelie smiled. "Great. That's a real milestone. He's making such big strides because of you."

"No. It has nothing to do with me, and everything to do with Colm himself."

Ceelie's smile faded. "So what's the problem, Anna?"

"He made a transfer mistake and ended up at the wrong stop."

"He's okay?"

Anna nodded. "He's fine. He did everything right. He called me, then waited for the next bus and asked for help."

Ceelie reached across the counter and patted her hand. "So why do you look like someone kicked a puppy."

"I feel like somebody did."

"Liam?" Ceelie guessed.

"Liam," Anna confirmed. "He wasn't happy at all. He blamed me and he had every right to. I've let things with him get out of hand. It's interfering with my working relationship with the family." Her relationship with Liam had influenced her decisions— that wouldn't do.

"Anna, that was Liam's fear talking. He was worried about his brother. You know that families are like that. That's why we're so important. We can look at our clients objectively."

"I'm afraid I can't with Colm. He's different. Special."

"And so is his brother," Ceelie said softly.

She didn't deny it. Ceelie would see right through her if she tried to fudge the facts. "I've never seen Liam so furious. Even that first day, he wasn't like this. He knew we were riding buses around town, but he didn't know Colm was going to try it on his own. I didn't tell him in advance. And if I'm honest, it was because I was afraid of how he'd react."

"Why?"

"Because things with us are—were— going so well. And…if you'd have seen how he treated me in the beginning, like some enemy…" She shrugged, not sure how to explain it. "Liam was finally starting to trust me, and I blew it. I lost all credibility."

"You weren't up front with him?" Ceelie frowned. "That's not like you, Anna. You don't change for relationships. You've told me over and over again how your mother has tried to change for men, or tried to change men. You've never been willing to compromise yourself in that way."

Anna confessed, "I thought it would be easier if I presented Liam with Colm's accomplishment after the fact. Then I planned to ease him into the idea of Colm getting a job."

"You still hadn't mentioned that?"

She could hear the surprise in Ceelie's voice. "No," she admitted.

"Or the housing?" Ceelie asked.

"No."

"Anna…" Ceelie let her name hang there.

"I know, I've made a mess of it."

"It will blow over." Ceelie didn't sound as sure. "You're fierce when you're fighting for your clients. You don't pussyfoot around. You charge in like a bull in a china shop. That's what I'm worried about. That you're trying to change who you are in order to have a relationship with someone. That's not like you."

"No, it's not. Maybe it's best if things don't blow over. Maybe it's time to end things with Liam." Even as she said the words, she felt a sense of loss. But losing Liam was better than losing herself.

Anna didn't want to think about it right now. Right now, she wanted to tackle something easier. Like a nervous neighborhood. Yes, protesting neighbors were easier to face than Liam Franklin.

"I will fix things with Liam tomorrow. As for our most pressing concern, what are we going to do about the house?"

"Anna, I—" Ceelie was interrupted by a sound that would make a thundering herd of elephants sound quiet. Thuds and scuffles, finally the remaining bits of a conversation.

"…and I'm going to tell her, 'cause you know you ain't supposed to…"

Enrico and Natalie, more commonly known as Nico and Nat, stopped short when they saw her. "Aunt Anna," they cried, pushing past each other in order to hug her.

They were eight and seven, respectively,

both with dark-brown hair bordering on black, and the most soulful brown eyes Anna had ever seen. Their father, Emmanuel, had left shortly after Natalie was born, and Anna had always marveled at how flawlessly Ceelie seemed to balance raising her children on her own with everything else she did. They had no family in the area, and Anna filled in as a surrogate aunt. There was nothing surrogate in her feelings for the kids. She adored them as much as they adored her.

She kissed the tops of their heads as they hugged her. "Oops, my lips slipped," she joked.

"Your lips always slip, Aunt Anna," Nat said with laughter in her voice.

"Yeah, your lips are the slippiest ever," Nico agreed. "But you gotta be careful they don't slip in front of the guys."

"Nico's guys are mean," Nat tattled. "They said I can't play baseball 'cause I'm a girl. And he said okay."

"Nico?" Ceelie asked.

"Mom, I know Nat's good at baseball, but the guys don't play with girls."

Anna could see how important fitting in with the guys was to Nico, but she could also see he felt guilty about hurting Nat's feelings. The two were closer than most siblings she'd known.

"Nico, I'm not going to make you take your sister." Ceelie's tone was gentle, without reproof or censure. "Everyone deserves to have some alone times."

"Oh yeah, you don't take us on dates," he said.

"That's true," Ceelie replied. "Although to be honest, you generally wouldn't be interested in my dates."

"Museums, blah," Nico graphically illustrated his feelings with a gagging motion.

"Yes, I know. You're not a big fan. But Nat *is* a fan of baseball. Still, I won't insist you take her, though. That's up to you."

"Ah, Mom."

"You can go without me, Nico. I don't want the guys to pick on you 'cause of me." Nat hugged her brother. "I won't bug you guys."

"Thanks, Nat," Nico said, as he ran out of the room.

"That was very understanding of you, Nat," Anna said.

"Nah. He's gonna go tell the guys to let me

play," she said with a little girl's confidence in her big brother.

"How do you know?" Anna asked.

"'Cause he loves me more than he likes them. I'd better go get my mitt."

"And if he doesn't come back?" Anna asked Ceelie.

"He will because Nat's right, Nico loves her more than he's worried about what the guys say." Ceelie paused, then added, "And Liam will get over his scare about Colm on the bus because he loves his brother more than he's worried about his own anxiety. He wants what's best for Colm, and it's obvious to anyone who knows you that you're what's best for him."

Anna felt a coil of tension that had twisted in her stomach begin to loosen thanks to Ceelie. "I hope you're right, but I can't do anything about it now. What I can do is work on what we're going to say in front of City Council. Maybe letters—testimonials—from neighbors of our two other homes?"

For the next fifteen minutes they talked strategies, and then Nico stormed into the kitchen. "Where's Nat?"

"Upstairs, I think."

"Okay. I'm gonna get her and take her with me. The guys said she could play, too."

Ceelie didn't comment on Nico's torn shirt or dirt-smudged face; she only nodded and said, "Well, that's nice of them. Be back before street lights come on, okay?"

"Sure, Mom." He sped back out, screaming, "Nat," at the top of his lungs.

"See, I was right about Nico, and I'm right about Liam. Don't worry."

Telling Anna not to worry…well, it was like telling Colm not to smile. Worry seemed to be coming as naturally to her as smiling came to him.

CHAPTER SEVEN

THE NEXT MORNING, Anna arrived promptly at Colm's. "Hi, Aunt Betty. How are things here?"

"You've got everything in a tizzy. Colm is upstairs packing a fanny pack for your bus ride for ice cream, and it's only 10:00 a.m. Meanwhile, Liam hasn't done more than grunt at me. He's in his office with the door shut." And in case Anna missed the significance, she said, "And he never shuts his office door."

"I know."

"And I'm not asking what happened between the two of you, but I hope you're over your lovers' tiff soon."

"I don't think there's anything between Liam and me anymore except Colm. And unfortunately, we disagree about what's best for him."

"So you had a fight," Aunt Betty stated.

Anna knew every couple disagreed and occasionally fought, but yesterday hadn't been a lovers' tiff. "It was more than that, Aunt Betty. And it was my fault. I should never have allowed myself to get involved with a client's relative." She glanced up the stairs. "I am sort of waiting for Liam to come and tell me I can't have Colm today."

Aunt Betty put her hands on her hips and shook her head. "He won't do that. He might be obstinate, but he's not stupid. Anyone can see how much you've helped Colm accomplish."

"But there's so much more he can do, and Liam—"

"Anna, you're a take-the-world-by-the-horns sort of woman."

Aunt Betty's words struck Anna as ironic since she'd been thinking of how carefully she'd been treading, trying not to upset Liam.

"Not everyone functions at full steam ahead," Aunt Betty continued. "Give Liam a bit of a breather. Let him catch up with you. You both have what's best for Colm in mind, and—"

Anna leaned forward and hugged the older

woman. It was uncharacteristic. Normally she wasn't nearly as demonstrative. Maybe Colm was rubbing off on her. She smiled at the thought. "Thanks."

Suddenly, Colm ran into the room and screamed, "Anna, I'm all ready!"

"Inside—"

"—voice, Colm," he supplied. "Okay, my inside voice says let's go catch the bus for ice cream."

"It's only ten o'clock. Are you sure you can eat ice cream at ten o'clock in the morning?"

Colm laughed. "I can eat ice cream anytime."

"Then let's go." She turned to Aunt Betty. "If Liam comes out will you tell him we should be back in an hour or so?"

"I'll tell him."

"And will you tell him I'd like a few minutes to talk to him? I need to make an apology." Maybe she needed to step back from this case? It would break her heart to go, but Ceelie could step in.

"I'll tell him that, too, sweetie. It will be all right. You'll see."

"Colm, are you ready?"

He patted his fanny pack. "Oh, yeah. I got

the phone you gave me, in case I get lost on the bus. And I got bus money. And—"

He continued cataloging the impressive list of items he'd brought for their excursion as they walked outside. Anna looked back at the house and thought she saw the curtains in Liam's office window move. She wasn't sure whether it was a breeze or he was watching. In case he was watching them, she gave a small wave in his direction.

"Let's go, Anna. You sure are slow…"

IT HAD BEEN an hour at least since Liam had lost sight of Colm and Anna, and he was still gazing out the window, waiting for them to come back. He presumed they had gone for ice cream. And had taken the bus, despite the fact the ice cream store was within walking distance.

He'd thought earlier about calling and telling Anna not to come, but in the end, he couldn't do it. Intellectually, he knew she was right. She was good for Colm. She had taught his brother so much in the past two months. He'd be selfish to take that away from Colm.

And yet, he wanted to.

He wanted things to stay the same.

He wanted to know that Colm was here, at home, safe, not out in Whedon, riding the bus on his own, being forced to deal with unkind people.

However, as much as he didn't like admitting it, it was true that he couldn't keep his brother in bubble wrap. He had to let Colm go out and become everything he could be. He had to give his brother the world, even if it meant some bumps and bruises along the way.

But he didn't have to like it.

And he could be pissed at Anna if he wanted.

Even as he had the thought, he realized that he didn't really want to be mad at her.

She just made him feel…

That was it. She simply made him feel. And he knew he had to man-up and apologize for yesterday. He'd known as he'd railed against her that she didn't deserve his anger. He couldn't pinpoint all the things he was mad about. It seemed that for as long as he could remember that anger was a part of him. Most of the time it merely smoldered in the background, and on a few occasions, like yesterday, it erupted.

Betty opened his door without knocking

and caught him still staring out the window. He felt embarrassed and he wasn't sure why.

"There you are, brooding." She crossed her arms over her ample chest and gave him the Betty-eye. It was very much akin to a mom-eye. It said things like straighten up, or stop pouting. Or brooding, as the case might be.

"I'm not brooding. I'm…" He wracked his brain for something. "I'm thinking. I've got a problem. A computer problem," he clarified. "And I need to think it through."

He glanced at his computer screen, which had long since gone to screen-saver mode. Pictures of Colm flashed one after another.

Betty nodded. "Yes. Thinking a problem through is always good. Trying to figure out why that problem happened is good, as well. Sometimes, what you think the problem is, it isn't really."

He didn't think Betty even knew how to send e-mail. "Oh? You've been studying computers?"

"No. I've studied you since you were a boy. And I know that you love your brother more than words can say. You've been good to him, taken care of him your whole life.

Like your parents did. And then here comes this woman, this outsider, who's made it clear your parents, you and me, we've all underestimated Colm. We didn't see how many things he could do. We saw his disability. Anna, she sees Colm. Not some medical label. She waltzes in here and starts turning everything topsy-turvy. You wouldn't be human if that didn't get to you."

He pointed at the computer. "Hey, we were talking about business problems."

"*You* were talking about business problems. *I* was talking about you. You and Anna. She would like to talk to you when she gets back with Colm. And I wanted to tell you that maybe she was wrong not to warn you. But let's face it, you fought against having her here and she was leery. So, you're wrong, too. And I'm as guilty as you about Colm. I feel horrible about it."

"You think we screwed up." He'd meant it to come out as a question, but instead it was a statement. He agreed. They'd all screwed up with Colm. "You think that we've hurt him?"

"I don't think you can hurt someone by loving them, Liam. And you love Colm and you know he deserves to go as far as he can go, even if it means he leaves us behind. And I believe that you're going to continue to let Anna work with him because you love him and you know she's good for him. For you, too, if you're not too pigheaded to admit it."

"Aunt Betty—"

She waggled a finger at him. "Don't Aunt Betty me, Liam Franklin. You sit up here and mull your problem over. And when Anna comes back with Colm you talk to her. Really talk to her. I trust you'll make the best decision for Colm."

She left, quietly shutting the door behind her.

Liam continued his mulling—hell, his brooding—until he saw Anna and Colm coming up the front steps.

Downstairs he found Colm telling Betty about his adventure. "…and Anna, she didn't say nothin'. I got us all the way to the ice cream store and back. I didn't get lost like yesterday. I did it perfectly." He spotted Liam. "Hey, Liam. I rode the bus again, but no mistakes this time. Anna was with me, but she didn't say nothin'. Maybe next time you can ride with us? You coulda today, but you had your door closed and Aunt Betty said not to bother you, so I didn't. But next time, you can leave the door open and then you can come, too."

"Next time I'll try to leave the door open," he promised. Liam looked at Anna, who wasn't meeting his eyes. "Hey, why don't you go with Aunt Betty a minute and let me talk to Anna."

"Okay. Anna, you tell him how good I did?"

She reached out and ruffled his hair. "I will, Colm."

As Colm went into the kitchen with Aunt Betty, Liam faced Anna. "About yesterday—"

She looked stubborn. "I am not going to apologize. Well, I am going to apologize for not talking to you about it first. I'm sorry about that part. That was cowardly of me. But about actually working toward a solo bus trip, I'm not apologizing. Colm was right. I didn't say a word about how to get to the ice cream store. He figured it out himself. He was never really in danger, Liam. I know you think you're protecting him, but—"

"I want to apologize." There, he'd said it and immediately felt lighter for it. "I'm sorry about yesterday. I was afraid, but rather than coming out as fear, it manifested as anger. It's easier to be angry than afraid. And you didn't deserve the way I acted. I'm very sorry."

She seemed surprised. "You are?"

He nodded. "I am."

"Oh."

He waited, thinking she was going to say more—he'd already learned that Anna almost always had more to say, but this time, she obviously didn't, because she was silent. "So, am I forgiven, or should I grovel?" he prompted.

She smiled. There was a hesitancy that hadn't been there before, and he hated that he'd been the one to put it there.

"Groveling is never necessary, Liam. You love Colm and you were worried. I get that. I was worried, too. I always am. I work with my clients and try to prepare them for every contingency, but still it's hard to let them go. And they're not my family, so I can only imagine how much worse it is for you."

She paused, then added, "I need to offer to step out of the picture, if you'd feel more comfortable. Ceelie, the other life coach at the foundation, she could fill in."

"I'm sure Ceelie is good at what she does," Liam said. And he was. But she wasn't Anna. Anna was the person Colm needed. The person *he* needed. "But I want you to keep working with Colm. Unless you'd prefer not to?"

"No, that's not what I prefer at all." She glanced at her watch. "I should find Colm and say goodbye. I need to get going."

On the surface things were okay, but Liam couldn't help but sense that they weren't. "Maybe we could go out to dinner tonight to celebrate?"

"I've got three other appointments this afternoon, but if you guys don't mind waiting…"

"We don't mind," he assured her.

"Uh, Liam, I hate to broach the subject and make you mad again, but I'd like to have a chat about Colm applying for that assistant's job at Keller's."

Liam wanted to shout no. To tell her that Colm didn't need a job, any more than he needed to know how to ride a bus. But even as he had the knee-jerk thought, he knew he couldn't voice it. "You said you had an interview set up. When?"

"Next week."

"I really don't know how I feel about it. So, I'm not saying yes to the job. But I will agree to the interview. Maybe he won't get hired." He tried to feel optimistic about the possibility, but couldn't quite manage it.

"You've met your brother. He's the most people-person person I've ever met." She laughed. "Okay, that was convoluted, but you know what I mean. There's no way he won't get the job. I want to be sure you're okay with it."

"I'm not, but I'm beginning to suspect that's my problem, not yours or Colm's. So, yes. Go ahead, let him apply and interview. Give me a chance to adjust, Anna. I'm trying."

Anna hugged him, her delight evident. "Thanks, Liam. You won't regret it."

He didn't tell her, but he knew that he already did.

ANNA HAD SESSIONS with Gabriella, then with Gilly and finally with Josh. It was a long day, but a good one. Gilly and Josh both lived at home with their parents, but they were both ready to be on their own. That's what the Trudy Street house was for—Josh and Gilly.

And maybe Colm. There would be 24/7 supervision at first, but Anna was confident that eventually that could be cut back.

She didn't doubt that Colm would fit in well with Gilly and Josh. He was a man who had been coddled and waited on for thirty years and was now coming into his own. Yes, she was pretty sure that by the time the house was ready, Colm could be.

She wasn't sure about Liam, though.

Not for the first time, Anna wished she could understand him better.

She parked in front of the Franklin house and stared at the porch. It reminded her of Colm. That porch was beautiful and had so much potential, but for years it had sat there, alone and neglected. She didn't want to see that happen to Colm. And regardless of her feelings for Liam, she was going to be more professional in her dealings with him about Colm.

She couldn't avoid telling him things because she didn't want to rock the boat. Her entire job description was one of boat-rocking.

Maybe it would be better to break things off with Liam and get back to a simple professional relationship.

But even as she had the thought, she discarded it.

Liam was sort of like the porch, too. Maybe with a little attention she could figure out what was going on with him. She wanted to know, to understand, not only for Colm's sake, but for their sake. She liked Liam more than anyone she'd met in a very long time.

There was a knock on her car window and she jumped.

She looked over and saw Liam smiling at her. She got out of the car and simply said, "Hi."

"You've been staring at my porch again."

She shrugged. "I finished my last appointment and was thinking."

"A bad one?" He started to lean in and kiss her, but then abruptly stopped, as if he wasn't sure what her reaction would be.

She noticed the aborted attempt, and reached out to take his hand. "No, it wasn't a bad day at all. It was a very good one as a matter of fact."

"I'm glad."

She got out of her car and joined him. "Listen, before we go inside, I need to tell you that part of me, the part that likes dating you, would like to stop pushing Colm. The other part, the professional part, won't— can't. So, I need to know if you can keep the professional separate from the personal, because it's not an option for me."

"I can try."

She gave his hand a squeeze. "Good. Trying is all I can ask."

"Good." He started to walk toward the house, still holding her hand.

She gave his hand a tug. "Hold on, one more thing. I want to let you know that I'm taking Colm to meet two other clients. I think he'd benefit from some friends. They all function on a similar level, though Josh is so quiet sometimes you don't know how much is going on in his head. I thought maybe we'd all take an outing next week."

If that went well, then she'd talk to him about the house. It wasn't her wimping out, it was just her giving him time to adjust.

Liam didn't say anything for a moment, then he nodded. "Thanks for letting me know."

"We're not going to fight?"

"No. Fighting with you is not what I have in mind."

He leaned down, as if he were going to kiss her, but Colm shouted, "Hey, Anna, Liam."

Liam pulled back and they both watched as Colm ran down to them. "Let's take Anna to Macky's to eat. We can ride the bus, and I can show you how good I am."

Anna looked at Liam. "What do you say? Do you want to see Colm in action?"

"Sure. Macky's sounds great."

Anna thought for a moment that Liam was going to say no. She could see that he wanted to. He wanted to keep everything the same. On one level, it made sense, on another, it just didn't. Still, she felt as if they'd come to some sort of an agreement about Colm. Maybe things would be smoother from here on out.

"WELL, THANKS FOR DINNER, Liam. I'd better get going. I have an early day tomorrow at the office. We have to put the finishing touches on a grant. I'll be by to get Colm after lunch. Probably about one." Anna was all business. Professional and polite. Informing him of her plans for the day.

Colm had already given her a hug and sprinted into the house.

"That's fine, Anna. You don't have to clear every step you make with me."

"Fine. See you then."

"Hey, hang on a minute."

She took another half step toward her car, then stopped and turned around. "Yes?"

"You're forgetting something."

"I am?"

"You're forgetting this." He kissed her then. At first, she held herself apart, stiff. But slowly she relaxed and moved further into his arms, her body pressed against his in all the right ways. When they eventually broke the kiss, he said, "I really am sorry."

"I am, too. I'm worried that somehow this—" She waved her hand between them. "That this will get in the way of my working with Colm and I don't want that, Liam. He has so much potential. I'm not saying this as a way of disparaging your family. What I am saying is that I care for Colm and want to help him go as far as he can."

"I know you do." And he'd have liked to have said he wanted that for Colm, too, but in his heart, he didn't. He wanted to keep Colm close and protect him. He knew it didn't make sense, but it was how he felt. Rather than saying that, he repeated, "I know you do, Anna. I think you and I can find a way to separate what we have and your job with my brother."

"And if we can't?"

He didn't have an answer for that.

It didn't surprise Liam at all. Seemed he didn't have an answer for a lot of things lately.

CHAPTER EIGHT

"I'M WORRIED," Ceelie said without preamble the following morning as Anna bounded into the office.

"Good morning to you, too," Anna said. "So what are we worrying about this morning? A kid? A client? The grant?"

"The grant's finished. If you'll just do a read-through, I'd appreciate it. I left it on your desk. And my kids are…well, they're bickering as always, but they're fine. My client-base is doing well. I'm worried about the house."

"Listen, we have the variance from the zoning board. And we'll just have to persuade those protesting neighbors. Our clients deserve to have homes. And even if the home would mean more than two non-family members in the house, I think they'll function as a family. I'm planning to take Colm over to meet Gilly and Josh this afternoon." She hoped they'd be roommates someday.

She'd promised she'd discuss things with Liam, and she would. As soon as she was sure that they all meshed. Before she could even seriously consider recommending Colm for housing there was still a lot to do. Colm getting a job being the big one.

"I am worried that if we can't make this new house happen, your heart will break. You've fought so hard for this one."

"It's my first attempt." And there was a sense of pride in the job she'd done.

"I know. And I'm worried about you in general."

"Ceelie, I'm fine. The house will be fine. We'll both be dancing when we've cleared that last hurdle and made our presentation to City Council."

"I keep thinking about when we were talking at my house. I know I said it would all be okay, but I think you've gotten too close to the Franklin brothers.

"I know there's no oversight, no rules against our seeing the people we work with, but Anna, I think this week has shown why there should be rules. I know I was all sunshine and it's-going-to-be-all-right the other night, but I don't know if you can serve Colm's needs as well as you should if you're this wrapped up in the whole family."

Anna knew her friend was right. But there was no keeping herself distanced from the Franklin brothers. And to be honest, she wasn't trying to. They touched her. And she thought she was good for them. "Ever since that first day, I've been wrapped up in the Franklins and I don't know how to unwrap," she admitted.

"Maybe you should try. You're going to end up hurt."

"Maybe, maybe not. But maybe this is where I'm supposed to be. Maybe…" She realized who she sounded like. Her mother. Believing in a relationship that had no chance of working out. Clinging to someone when everyone else was warning her to let go.

The thought was uncomfortable.

"You're getting too close, too fast, Anna."

"With Colm, not Liam." That was a lie.

Ceelie was far too much of a mom to buy

that. "Maybe with Colm, but with Liam, too. And from what you've told me, he's not an easygoing sort of guy."

"Ceelie, I have everything under control. Colm's riding the bus now on his own. I'm taking him for a job interview on Monday, and…" She paused, afraid she was sounding too defensive. "It's good, Ceelie. It's all good."

"I hope so, Anna. For your sake, and for Colm's."

Anna noticed Ceelie didn't include Liam. She realized that Liam had probably had that happen his whole life—people worried about Colm, but not for him.

The thought broke her heart.

AFTER LUNCH, Anna pulled the van up in front of Colm's. He was sitting on the porch next to Aunt Betty and bolted for the van as soon as it stopped.

He opened the door and poked his head in. "Where we goin', Anna?"

"I thought you might like to meet a couple of my friends."

"Okay." He climbed into the passenger

seat, shut the door and buckled his seatbelt. "Are they nice?"

"I'm pretty sure all my friends are nice, Colm. I thought the four of us could have a bit of an adventure today."

"Are we taking the bus?"

"Not this time. We're going to take this van because my friend Josh is in a wheelchair, and the van is easier for him than my car or a bus." She started toward Gilly's house.

Anna glanced over at Colm and he was frowning. "Oh. Why's your friend in a wheelchair?"

Josh's story wasn't hers to share, and Anna wasn't sure she would even if she could. She answered, "Because his legs don't work right. But he's very, very nice. I think you'll like him."

"And the other guy?"

"Is Gilly. I think you'll like him, too. He tells knock-knock jokes."

Rather than looking relieved, Colm looked worried. "Do you think they'll like me? Most guys don't, 'cept Liam, and he has to 'cause he's my brother. But these guys might not."

Everything in her wanted to assure Colm that of course Josh and Gilly would like him, but he deserved more than hollow promises on her part. She thought they would all three connect. As a matter of fact, she was counting on it. But there was no reasoning out chemistry. It was either there, or it wasn't. "Colm, we can't control how other people feel or behave. All we can do is be in charge of ourselves. So, even if they don't like you, you should be kind."

"Yeah, lots of people didn't like me in school, and I was still nice. But Liam, he had fights. I don't want you to have fights if these guys don't like me, Anna."

"Liam was young in school. He's older now, and he doesn't have fights anymore, does he?" she asked. She knew that even though Liam no longer got in physical fights on Colm's behalf, he'd do whatever Colm needed him to do.

"Nah, he don't fight no more."

"See? You don't need anyone fighting for you. You can handle yourself."

"What if someone's mean? They call me names sometimes," he said in a whisper.

"If someone's mean, then you need to feel sorry for them because they have…"

"Small hearts?" he asked, obviously remembering their last conversation.

"Yes."

"And that must hurt."

Anna nodded. "I think having a small heart must hurt a lot. You're special, Colm. No one can take that away from you by calling you a mean name."

"Yeah. But I'm not smart like Liam."

"You're different than Liam. You're different than anyone else in the world. You're Colm, and that's special enough."

"I'm special different?" He laughed, happy again.

"You're very special different. So are Gilly and Josh."

"Maybe if we're all different, that makes us the same and they'll like me."

Anna felt her heart constrict and she hoped that the three men would become friends. Colm could use some friends. And maybe, if the house was rezoned, maybe the three of them…

She was getting ahead of herself.

She'd have to broach the idea with Liam slowly. But she wouldn't hide the idea this time. She knew Colm could do it. She'd present her well-thought-out reasons. Logically. And trust that logic and his love for his brother would win out.

Sunrise's goal was to help clients live up to their full potential, to be as independent as possible. And Colm had so much untapped potential. Anna wanted to help him live an adult life on his own. A life that included a job, friends, his own home. He was a grown-up, not a child. And he deserved what all her clients deserved—Anna's complete commitment to him and helping him find out how far he could go.

She couldn't do that if she worried about fighting with Liam.

Ceelie was right that getting involved with Liam had been a mistake. She normally had no trouble fighting for what her clients needed. But fighting against Liam was harder because…

Because she cared for him.

She cared for him and she cared for Colm.

Liam wanted the status quo. He didn't want things to change.

But Colm deserved to live the life that he could.

What was best for Colm and what Liam thought was best for himself were two different things. Somehow Anna was going to have to find a balance and do what was best for everyone.

The ride to Gilly's house wasn't long. He was waiting for them as well and climbed into the van. "Gilly, this is Colm Franklin. Colm, this is Gilbert Masters."

Gilly thrust out a hand. "Come on, fella, you gotta shake when you're a guy and meet another guy." He took Colm's hand in his and pumped it up and down. "There. That's how us guys do it. But don't call me Gilbert. Call me Gilly. Everyone does. Except my aunt. She calls me Gilbert. And she won't shake. She hugs. And she smells funny. Mom says I have to be a man and hug her anyway. But guys, we can shake."

"I'll remember that. Anna, she never taught me that." Colm shot her a look that said she should have.

Gilly shook his head and looked serious as he proclaimed, "Yup, Anna's good, but she's still a girl."

"Hey, Gilly, I'm right here." Anna waved

her hand for emphasis. "Why don't you get buckled up so we can go get Josh?"

Gilly snickered as he buckled. "Sorry, Anna." He dropped his voice to a stage whisper and said, "You gotta be careful of girls, Colm. They get their feelings hurt real easy, Dad says."

Anna started back toward I-79 for Route 6N. Then they swung toward Waterford to pick up Josh.

"You live with your mom and dad?" Colm asked.

"For now. But Anna's looking for a house for me and Josh. We've been working real hard, me and him, so that we can get our own place. And then we'll be the bosses. My mom makes me clean up my clothes and maybe in my own house I won't."

"Come on, Gilly," Anna said. "Who wants to step on dirty clothes? If you get your own place, you'll still need to pick up."

"See, that Anna, she's a girl like my mom." Gilly's tone said that Anna and his mom's girliness was not a huge compliment.

Colm ignored the discussion of dirty clothes on the floor and instead asked,

"You're gonna live with Josh, not your mom and dad?"

"Yeah. Hey, who d'you live with?" Gilly asked.

"My brother, Liam."

"Ah, that's tough, guy. Livin' with a brother ain't the same as livin' with a friend. Me and Josh, we're gonna have a guys' house."

"Me and Liam have a guys' house."

"But it's not the same if it's your brother," Gilly said sadly.

Anna decided it was time to change the subject. "Gilly, Colm is going to talk to a man about a job on Monday. Why don't you tell him about your job at the warehouse."

"Oh, man, my job is so cool, Colm. We get all these glasses and you have to be real careful so you don't break 'em. Then we wrap 'em and…"

Gilly's step-by-step account of his job took them all the way to Josh's house. Josh was on the porch with his foster mom, waiting for them. He waved when he saw the van.

"Oh, here comes Josh, Colm," Gilly announced. "You're gonna like 'im. He don't say too much, but he's a good guy."

Anna lowered the lift on the side of the van and strapped Josh's chair in. She had become an expert at strapping the chair into the van. "Josh, this is Colm Franklin. Colm, this is Josh Hampton."

Thanks to Gilly's tutelage, Colm thrust out his hand to shake.

"No, Colm," Gilly said before Anna had a chance to. "Josh's hands don't work so good, like his legs don't. So me and him we do a fist bump. Anna taught us. Like this." He bumped his fist to Josh's and Colm followed suit.

Josh simply smiled.

"Okay, everyone's buckled in and set. Let's go to the zoo."

"Better watch out, Colm. Last time we went to the zoo, Anna started singing and—"

Right on cue, she started singing Tom Paxton's "Going to the Zoo."

"See, Colm, that Anna, she's crazy." But despite his decree, Gilly was soon singing along, and it didn't take Colm long until he'd caught on to enough of the chorus to sing as well. She glanced back into the rearview mirror and saw Josh grinning.

Anna felt a sense of satisfaction. She'd thought these three might hit it off, and it looked as if she was right.

IN BETWEEN conference calls introducing Ben to clients he'd be taking over, Liam spent his day speculating what Anna and Colm were doing.

It was quickly apparent that Ben wasn't only well-versed with computers, he had people skills, as well.

Aunt Betty had already left for the day and the house was quiet. It should have made work whiz along. Instead, the silence seemed oppressive. Liam finally put a CD on.

When Anna brought Colm back, he felt a sense of relief. He wasn't sure why he'd been anxious. He knew Anna would look out for Colm. As he listened to his brother's account of the outing, Liam's nerves finally relaxed.

"…and then we picked up Josh. Anna, she was drivin' the van, 'cause he's in a wheelchair. His hands don't work so good neither, so he can't shake like Gilly, but he fist-bumps like this."

Colm bumped Liam's hand.

"I liked 'em," Colm said with a huge, happy sigh.

"I'm glad." As Colm had given his rundown of the day's events, what stood out the most for Liam was that Colm had been lonely. How could he not have known that? Everyone needed people in their lives. And as he had the thought, he realized that so much of his life was wrapped up in work and Colm that he hadn't cultivated many real friendships either. He had neighbors, colleagues and now Ben, a coworker. He had Aunt Betty and Anna, though he suspected there was a growing distance between himself and Anna. He glanced at her. Her hair was in a ponytail and she had on a baseball cap. She was smiling as she listened to Colm.

"Yeah, I got friends now," his brother said. "They don't call me names or nothin'. And Anna, she knows like *everything* about the zoo. She's gonna take me to talk to a guy about a job. My friend Gilly, he has a job and he told me all about it."

"Why don't you get cleaned up for dinner, bud?" Liam said.

"That's a good idea, 'cause I touched lots of stuff and my hands smell funny." He thrust a hand toward Liam's nose. "Wanna smell?"

Liam took a step back. "No, that's okay. You go wash. I want to talk to Anna a minute."

Colm disappeared noisily up the stairs.

They both watched Colm's retreat, then Anna turned to Liam and asked, "So, what did I do now?"

"Nothing. I didn't get rid of him to have another fight. This is about what I'm going to do…" And he pulled her into his arms and kissed her. "There. I feel better now."

She laughed the way she might have before Colm rode the bus, but Liam thought he detected a difference in the sound. It was more restrained. Still, she snuggled close and said, "Me, too."

"I don't like fighting with you."

"Me, neither. And to avoid any possible miscommunication, I'm taking Colm for that interview on Monday next week."

Liam reminded himself that it was what was best for Colm. And he wanted what was best for his brother, so this was a good thing. "Okay."

"Okay? That's it?" She looked up at him and smiled.

"I didn't say yes to the job, only to the interview," he reminded her.

Her happy expression faded and Liam felt bad. "But you and I both know that if he gets it, I'll agree. No matter what you think, I do want what's best for him."

She buried her head into his chest. "I know that, Liam."

He wished he could see her expression, so he broke off the hug. "Tell me how it would work."

"When a client gets a job, we stay with them. We'd probably start off slow. Only mornings or afternoons. Just a few hours a day. I'd be right there next to him until he felt comfortable."

"What would he do?"

"He'd probably start with small things. Mopping. Bringing in carts. Packing shopping bags. Zac Keller, who runs the grocery store, is a nice guy. He's been involved in other community initiatives, and he's willing to find what the best situation is for Colm. When Colm gets a check, I'd probably take him to the bank and open an account for him. That would lead to lessons in economics, on saving—"

Liam nodded. "I've noticed that. Everything leads to a lesson, that leads to another lesson."

"Tailoring our teaching to our clients' needs, that's what we're about."

"I'm not a client, but I wondered if you'd consider giving me a lesson. There's one I'd like to try—"

Colm came barreling down the stairs. "Okay, guys, I'm all cleaned. Yep, I cleaned the mess great. Wanna play some Go Fish?"

Anna looked at Liam, he nodded and was rewarded by a smile. It wasn't exactly what he'd had in mind, but he was spending time with Anna. That was all that mattered.

ANNA WAS MORE NERVOUS than Colm on Monday at the interview. She thought she was doing a pretty good job of hiding it, but wasn't sure she was really successful, or if it was only wishful thinking. She really wanted this to be a good fit for Colm.

"Hi," she said to a beautiful young blonde at the customer service desk. "My name's Anna Chapel and this is—"

"Hi, I'm Colm." He thrust out his hand, and the girl smiled and shook it. "My friend Gilly, he said you should shake hands."

The girl smiled and shook his hand. "I'm Ariel. And Mr. Keller said to show you to his office when you arrived."

"Yeah, I'm gonna go meet him and get a job here," Colm said as Ariel led them toward the back of the market. Anna followed behind them. "I'm gonna be very good. Maybe you could get a job here, too."

"I already work here, Colm," Ariel told him. "Mr. Keller gave me a job last year when I was going to have a baby. I'm in college now, and I still work here."

"You gotta baby?" Colm asked.

"Yes, a little girl. Her name is Nora. Sometimes she comes to work with me. I'm sure you'll meet her."

"Oh, I like babies, but I promise, I'll be careful. There was a lady once and she had this baby in a stroller and I went "Hiya, baby" and was goin' to pat its head, but the lady she screamed and said to be careful, but I was bein' careful. Liam said I can't touch no babies like that, so I won't, but I'd sure like to meet Nora."

Ariel glanced over at Anna and she could see the girl was moved.

"Colm, we've only just met, but I can tell right away that you'd be very careful with my baby. When you meet her, you can hold her if you like."

"Really? You'd let me hold her?"

Ariel nodded. "Really. And Mr. Keller, he has a baby, too. Johnny's about Nora's age."

"Man, I really like babies."

"And I bet they love you, Colm." Ariel stopped in front of a door at the very back corner of the store. "This is it. Good luck. And you come find me if you need anything, Colm."

She strode toward the front of the store and Colm looked at Anna. "Hey, Anna, I think I got another friend. Ariel said I could hold her baby. I promise I'll be real careful, and I won't touch no babies unless their moms say so."

"I'm pretty sure you do have another friend, Colm. Now, are you ready?"

"Sure."

Anna was going to knock, but Colm beat her to it.

A voice called, "Come in," and without

any hesitation, Colm walked into the office. "Hi, I'm Colm. And I wanna work here. I'm friends with Ariel already, and she said I could hold her baby. I like babies, but if I work here, I won't touch none unless moms say I can, 'cause moms they worry a lot."

Zac Keller was an average-looking guy. Brown hair, maybe four or five inches taller than she was. But he grinned as Colm's speech wound down, and went from average to absolutely gorgeous that quick. "Well, it seems you've been busy."

Colm nodded. "Yeah, I'm very busy. I know I'm different, but Anna says that's special. I can learn all kinds of stuff and I can work really hard."

"Why don't you both sit down," Zac offered.

Colm ran to a vacant chair and sat down, Anna took the other chair more slowly.

"I hear you got a baby, too," Colm said. "I bet he's really cute. We don't got no babies at my house. There's me and my brother Liam. He works, and we're twins, so I should work, too 'cause I wanna be like Liam. And I really wanna work here with Ariel and meet her baby."

"Well, that about says it all, Colm. Let me tell you a bit about what you'll be doing. At first, you can come in during the mornings and learn the ropes."

"You guys got ropes?" Colm asked.

"No. It means learn how we do things. We'll start you out with getting carts from the parking lot and bringing them in. Maybe sweeping some floors and wiping up spills when we have them."

"Oh, I'm really good at spills. Anna, she says, if you make a mess, clean it up, so I'm your cleanin' man."

Zac smiled. "It sounds like you're going to work out fine. We can have you start tomorrow. If that works for you."

Anna had known from her earlier conversation with Zac that Colm probably would be successful in getting the job, but still she felt a rush of excitement. "He's got the job?"

"He's got the job. I have a feeling Colm is going to be a very good addition to the Keller's Market family."

"I'm gonna work tomorrow?" Colm asked.

Zac nodded. "Yes. How about I call Ariel and she can give you a quick tour of the store?"

"Oh, yeah, she'll help me. She said she would. She's my friend. I didn't have any friends before, just Liam and Aunt Betty, but now I got all kinds of friends."

Colm chattered excitedly until Ariel came to get him.

As they left, Anna turned to Zac. "I can't thank you enough for giving Colm a chance."

"Anna, it's my pleasure. Keller's Market has always been a family store. And in my family, that means giving everyone a chance. I think Colm's going to be a real asset. He's certainly got an outgoing personality. Our customers are going to love him."

"I'm pretty sure you're right. He's special."

They talked about the details. Anna explained how her support would work. They laid out specific goals for Colm.

At the end of their meeting, Anna stood. "Thanks so much, Zac. Colm and I will see you tomorrow."

Out in the store, Anna found Colm wearing a Keller's Market shirt. "Look, Anna, I got a shirt. A special one that says I work here. Ariel showed me everything. And I got a lot of new friends."

Ariel smiled. "I'll see you soon, Colm."

Colm ran over and hugged the girl. There was no hesitancy in Ariel as she hugged him back.

"See you soon, Ariel." He took Anna's hand. "Come on, Anna. Let's go find Liam and tell him I got a job, too. And a shirt. His job don't have no cool shirts like this. Do you think he'll feel sad? Maybe we could buy him a cool shirt?"

There was a K-Mart just down the street and Anna grinned. "That's a lovely idea."

LIAM WAS on the porch wearing a brand new neon-blue T-shirt and listening to Colm. "…and I got you blue 'cause you don't got no cool work shirt and I didn't want you to feel bad, so look, it almost matches."

He held his shirt next to the sleeve of Liam's. A sedate royal blue next to an eye-blinding one. "Yes, they're both blue."

"Okay, well, I gotta go find Aunt Betty and tell her. She's gonna be so happy, ain't she?"

Colm didn't wait for an answer. He flew into the house hollering "Aunt Betty," at the top of his lungs.

"You're really okay?" Anna asked.

"How could I be anything but okay when I can see how happy he is?"

Liam ignored the worry-induced acid in the pit of his stomach. He was happy for Colm, but he was also worried. There were so many things that could go wrong. So many ways he could be hurt. Liam was positive that Anna would look out for him, but eventually Anna was going to leave and Colm would be on his own.

Liam didn't want to think about that.

"Do you want to celebrate tonight? How about Mexican and a movie?" Anna offered.

"Sure, I'm in. And I can't imagine Colm will complain."

No, he was pretty sure that Colm wouldn't complain about anything. His brother was happy.

Liam was going to focus on that.

CHAPTER NINE

THE FIRST WEEK at Keller's Market was a busy one. And it wasn't long before Anna had that bone-deep sense of contentment, a certainty, that this was going to be a good match, both for Colm and for Keller's Market. Colm's unflagging good nature seemed to appeal to the customers. "Hi," he'd call and wave as he gathered carts in the parking lot.

Anna found it hard to believe it was Friday and Colm was almost done.

They were working in the lot, talking about traffic safety. "Okay, here's an important lesson in the grocery business—the customer is always right. Even when they're not."

Colm stopped. "Huh?"

Anna gave a nod and he started pushing carts again. "If a customer makes a mistake—

like not putting their cart away—we don't yell at them because they might get upset and not shop here again. That would hurt Mr. Keller. And if someone's being mean, we can't say, 'Hey, you're being mean,' we can simply try to help them. Everything we do is supposed to make the customer feel good about shopping here. We smile, we say hi— like you're doing—and we help the customers whenever we can. If you see someone having trouble loading their groceries in their car, you can offer to help. Or—"

"Or if they leave their cart in the wrong place, I just smile and get it myself." He nodded as if to say this new rule made things clearer, then he pushed his three carts onto the long line of carts he'd already collected.

"That's right," Anna said. "The customer is always right."

"Okay." He turned and scanned the lot for more carts, then pointed. "See that lady over there? She's kinda old, and might need some help."

"Well, we never, ever tell a lady she's old—she might not like that. But you can go offer to help. That would be nice."

"And it would make her like Mr. Keller's store. Okay." He took off across the lot toward the lady in question.

"Look both ways," Anna called.

Colm shot her a look that said of course he knew that. With exaggerated caution he looked both ways, then walked up to the older woman and with great care put the bags in her trunk for her. They exchanged some words, Colm took her empty cart and brought it over to Anna.

"That was great, Colm. You definitely did a good job. You've really learned a lot this week."

"What's your job, Anna?"

"My job is helping you until you feel comfortable doing stuff on your own." And as she said the words, Anna realized that Colm wouldn't need her much longer. In the last few months he'd come so far. Faster than almost all her other clients. It was as if he'd simply been waiting for someone to show him what to do.

"Oh, okay. That's a good job, Anna. Later, Vic said he's gonna teach me to mop and pick up stuff. 'Gotta keep the store clean, Colm,' he said. Hey, here he is…"

"Hi, Colm," Vic said.

Vic took a broom and a dustpan with a long handle and showed Colm how to sweep up the litter in the parking lot. Anna sat down on a bench in the shade and watched them work.

"He's doing good then?" Liam asked as he sat down next to her.

Anna turned and couldn't help but smile. Things with Liam had been better. They'd gone all week without butting heads. He seemed to be adjusting to the idea of Colm working. "Spying, Mr. Franklin?" she teased.

"I was in the neighborhood."

She stared at him, waiting.

Finally, Liam laughed. "Okay and maybe spying a little, too. I worry. I know, it's not manly to admit it."

"Hey, having a guy who cares as much as you do is every woman's dream. And when you care that much, worry is part of the package."

"So, how's he doing really? I know you've painted a glowing picture at home every night. Today's the end of his first week, and I wondered."

Wondered, not worried. That was progress.

Maybe she was making major progress with both Franklin brothers. "Honestly, I was sitting here thinking that I'm going to be obsolete here a lot sooner than I anticipated."

"And everyone's been kind?" There was worry again in Liam's voice.

Anna understood where it was coming from and reached out and took his hand. "Colm is already a hit. I suspect he's going to be one of the customers' favorite Keller's employees soon. Your brother is a bit of a flirt. No woman can resist his smile. He does it so often. It's too bad his brother doesn't do it more often."

"I think all Colm's smiling has something to do with you." Liam gave her hand a squeeze. "And his brother's smiled a lot more often since you've been around, too."

Anna felt a tingle of happiness. Liam did seem happier than he had the day they'd met. And if she had anything to do with that, she was pleased. "Ah, when I'm not making you crazy, I make you smile?"

"Something like that." He reached across the bench and played with one of her stray curls. "Any chance we could go out on a date sometime soon?"

She smiled and gave his hand a squeeze. "I think the chances are pretty good. What do you have in mind?"

"A friend has a boat docked on Lake Erie. I thought we could spend an afternoon out on the lake."

Anna loved Lake Erie, though she normally only got to visit its shores, not go boating on it. "That sounds lovely. I've taken the tour boat out onto the lake, but never a real boat that I could hang out on."

"I'll talk to him and see when it's available." He gave her a look that melted her. "The sooner the better."

It took a moment for Anna to find her voice again. "Just let me know."

"Anna, thanks for everything you've done with Colm. I should have said it sooner. I should have said it more often— say it more often."

"Are you feeling any better about everything?" she couldn't help but ask.

"I still worry. Obviously. Otherwise, why would I be here spying?" He smiled at his admission. "But I do think he's happier. He's more sure of himself. Thanks to you."

"Thanks."

Colm came running up to them and threw himself at Liam, giving him a brief hug. "Oh, man, Liam, did you see me working? I got the carts and I picked up junk in the parking lot. People are pigs, Vic says, but we can't say that to them 'cause the customer is always right, even if they're pigs, right, Anna?"

Anna stifled a chuckle. "Right, Colm." Of course, the words he'd uttered were loud enough that anyone in their vicinity would have heard his proclamation.

"I'm all done here, Liam. I've been working real hard, and that makes a guy hungry. Anna's been following me around, but not working, but I guess she'd be hungry, too."

"I am," she confirmed. She looked at Liam and knew that her hunger didn't have much to do with food.

"We should get lunch, right? You can wait here, Anna. Vic'll help me put stuff away and do my card thing, but I think I can do that by myself already." He looked at Vic for confirmation.

The older man nodded. "Sure, bud, come on with me."

Colm fell into step with Vic, and the man patted his shoulder.

"Bud. That's what Liam calls me. 'Hey, bud. Come here, bud.' I like it."

Vic chuckled. "I'm glad. I'm sure I'll call you that a lot. It's my word."

"I don't have a word. Maybe I should…" His voice faded as they entered the grocery store.

"I think that was Colm's polite way of firing me from coming to work with him," Anna said. "Actually, I think it may be time to cut back my sessions with Colm. He'll be busy here now, and there's not much more he needs from me."

"You know, despite the fact I wasn't excited when you started coming over, I find I'm equally not excited to hear you won't be."

"I'll still be by to work with Colm, only not as often. Maybe one day a week? He still has more things to learn, and I'd like to help him," she paused, then added, "if that's okay with you?"

"It's only okay with me if you'll come over more often for non-work reasons."

Anna smiled and slid closer to Liam. They sat on the bench, thigh touching thigh, arm touching arm. It felt good. Right.

"I think I could be convinced to spend more non-work time with you." Separate business from pleasure, she reminded herself. "And I wanted to check with you about Colm. I'd like him to spend more time with Gilly and Josh, too. They really hit it off."

"Sure. I'm glad he's got friends." Liam was staring at her with a glassy quality to his eyes.

Since Liam seemed in such a good mood, and so comfortable with Colm's growing autonomy, maybe this was a good time to talk to him about Colm eventually living on his own. "Uh, I think he could use friends, and I want to discuss—"

Liam didn't wait to hear what she wanted to discuss. As a matter of fact, talking seemed to be the furthest thing from his mind as he leaned over and kissed her. Not a deep, embarrassing-in-public sort of kiss, but rather a nice buss on the lips that was filled with the promise of something more intimate.

"Sorry, I couldn't help myself." Liam's grin belied his apology. He looked way too pleased with himself.

All thoughts of Colm and serious discussion fled. The only thing Anna could think about was an upcoming date with Liam.

THE NEXT WEEK went by as fast as the previous one.

Liam took Anna on their solo date on the lake. Her hair went wild in the wind.

And when he'd taken her below deck and made love to her, her hair fanned out on the bed, wild and alive.

He wasn't sure why he was thinking of that now, as he stood, unnoticed in the hallway, watching Anna with Colm in the kitchen. He loved seeing how she was with his brother. She brought out the best in Colm.

And if he was being truthful, she brought out the best in him as well.

"…You know, Colm, it's very kind of you to offer to take out the garbage," Anna said, as she stirred whatever she was making on the stove.

Colm was sitting on a stool at the island, pushing at what appeared to be a bunch of dough. "You do what you can."

"That's a new saying," Anna said.

"Yeah, Vic at work says it lots. He helped me the other day when someone knocked down boxes of crackers and I had to restack 'em, and he came over and helped and I said thanks, and he said—"

"You do what you can?" Anna guessed.

Colm look surprised that she knew. "Yeah, that's right, Anna. Vic, he says that everyone has things they do good. Me and him, we're good stackers, only he's good at numbers, too, and helps Mr. Keller with adding all our store's numbers up, but he's good at boxes, too."

"He's a nice man."

Liam remembered meeting Vic last week. He'd have to make sure and thank him next time he saw him.

"Yeah, he's real nice. I helped him carry some boxes in, and he said, 'Thanks, bud.' He likes me."

"That was very nice of you, Colm." That was the thing about Colm, he was all heart. "And of course he likes you. You're very nice."

"Hey, you do what you can." He laughed, and Anna did, too.

That was the sound that had filled the house since Anna had come into their lives. Suddenly, Liam could see her here permanently. He'd always thought having a serious relationship would be hard, since very few women would want to take on Colm. But that wouldn't be a problem for Anna.

It was early in their relationship, but for the first time in his life, Liam could see a potential future with a woman.

Not any woman—with Anna.

"So how was work, other than restacking the crackers?" she asked.

Colm didn't immediately answer, which was unusual. Liam looked at his brother and his normal jovial expression had turned sad.

"Did something happen, Colm?" Anna asked quietly.

"Yeah, these kids came in and I was moppin' up some water by the carts and they said, 'Hey, look at the retard.'"

Rage filled Liam where moments before he'd felt nothing but a warm glow. It was the same rage that had made him stand up to Bartle on the bus all those years ago. This feeling was an old friend. He'd spent his whole life with it burning in the background.

"So what did you say?" Anna asked.

Liam was ready to sweep in and say something. And the something he very much wanted to say was that agreeing to let Colm take this job had been a mistake. It was obvious that this job would only end up hurting Colm. But Colm started to answer.

"I told them yeah, that was one word, but it wasn't a nice one. Then I told 'em what you said. That I'm different, but I'm a special different. And special's not bad, it's just different."

"Everyone's different from everyone else. And when the different we're talking about is Colm Franklin, it is definitely a special thing." Liam watched as Anna squeezed Colm's hand. "Good for you, sticking up for yourself that way."

Colm laughed. "Yeah, they were just kids and probably didn't know better. Maybe next time they will, huh?"

"I hope so, Colm."

"A couple of the kids laughed when they left the store, but the one guy, he turned around so the other guys didn't see and gave me a smile. I think he'll remember."

"And that's a good start."

It wasn't a good start, Liam wanted to yell. What if Colm had been collecting carts and the kids had started in on him? What if no one was around to stop them from attacking Colm? Liam had promised his parents he'd look after Colm. He could keep him safe, here in the house, but out there? He had no control.

"Hey, Anna?" Colm said.

Anna stopped stirring. "Yes, Colm?"

"You're special, too."

She started blinking and Liam suspected it was to keep tears from falling.

"Thanks."

"You've been sad, and I thought maybe you forgot you were special, too."

Anna hugged him. "You're right. Sometimes I do forget, so thanks for reminding me."

Liam saw the second she spotted him. She didn't tell Colm he was there, instead she said, "Are you going to take that garbage out?"

Colm laughed. "Sure, Anna. I'm good at taking the garbage out. Vic says when I'm workin' no one's garbage can ever get too full, 'cause I keep an eye on 'em." Colm picked up a garbage bag and took it out the back door. As soon as he was gone, Liam stepped into the kitchen.

"How long were you there?" she asked.

"Long enough to have heard Colm's story

from work. Do you still maintain that this job is the best thing for him? Do you know what could have happened? There were times at school when words weren't enough. Kids tripped Colm, or knocked his books out of his hands. He never seemed to realize they'd done it on purpose, but I did."

"And you beat them all up?" she asked.

"Not all, but enough that eventually they stopped." He'd wanted to beat them all up. Every single kid who treated his brother poorly.

"Maybe Colm needed you then, but he didn't need you today, Liam. He handled it. All by himself. Without hitting anyone. He handled it by being himself. By being Colm. You heard the part about kids being cruel, I heard the part about Colm standing up for himself."

"I've spent my whole life taking care of Colm, and—"

"And you're having trouble standing back and accepting that Colm can take care of himself. Liam, you treat him as if he's profoundly handicapped. He's not. He takes a little longer to learn things than you or I might, but he learns. He deserves—"

"He deserves not to be hurt, not to be called names. He deserves—"

Colm burst back in the door. "Okay, Anna, I took it out and I put the lid on the garbage can real tight so no cats can get into it and make a mess." He flew at Liam, enveloping his brother in a hug. "Hi, Liam."

"Hi, Colm."

"I'm glad you're home, 'cause I did the shopping for Aunt Betty and Anna and me are makin' spaghetti for dinner. It's gonna be sooo—" he drew the word out "—good, 'cause it's my special…"

"Specialty," Anna filled in.

"Specialty. I make it great."

Colm went on talking about his day at work. He didn't mention the kids to Liam, but talked about Vic, Ariel and Mr. Keller. He talked about his favorite bus driver on the ride home. "And I said, hey Carl, knock-knock. He knew the game all by himself and said, 'Who's there, Colm?' And I said, Colm's not there, the bus was and he laughed. He likes knock-knock jokes."

Liam tamped down his anger and laughed on cue. Later he'd try to sort out who he was mad at. The kids who'd called his brother names, certainly, but Anna, too. She wouldn't listen, and he didn't know how to express all his fears for Colm without her dismissing them.

Liam knew he couldn't stand to see Colm hurt. Not when it was his job to protect his brother.

Liam wasn't sure what to do. He sat in the kitchen, listened to Colm chatter about his day as he weighed his options. He wished he could talk to Anna, but he knew what she'd say and he wasn't sure he wanted to hear it.

She'd tell him that Colm needed to be out in the world learning new things. And in his head, he knew she was right.

But in his heart, he knew it was his job to watch out for Colm and that on days like today, he knew he'd failed.

Anna had thought they were going to fight last week when Liam found out that Colm had been picked on at work, but they hadn't. On the surface, everything seemed the same. But Anna sensed that things had altered, and not for the better. Liam seemed distant and when she tried to ask him about it, he brushed off her concerns, telling her it was fine. *Everything was fine.* She didn't believe him, but didn't know what to do about it.

So, instead of worrying about Liam, she was concentrating on the moment. And today had been a particularly good one. She'd taken Colm, Gilly and Josh on another outing, and they'd had such a good time. Last week, Liam had been out of town on the Fourth of July, so she'd taken Colm, Gilly and Josh to Wyndham Park for the fireworks. Today, they'd gone to Presque Isle. There was a handicapped-accessible beach with a wooden boardwalk, so that Josh could maneuver in his wheelchair. They'd spent a great day in the sun, feeding seagulls and watching the waves pummel the shore.

Despite her worry about Liam, Anna knew she had to talk to him soon about the possibility of Colm eventually moving into a group home with Gilly and Josh. She was sure they'd get along well.

She was still mulling over how to handle it when she brought Colm home. Liam's office door had been closed, so they'd waited until he came down. By then, Colm was practically bursting with excitement.

"The door was closed," he complained. "I wanted to tell you 'bout the beach."

"Sorry, bud. I was on a business call and needed the quiet." Liam mussed Colm's hair then took a seat at the kitchen counter. "But I'm here now."

"Yeah, you're here now. So's me and Anna. We went to the beach, but first we got Josh and Gilly. We took the van again, 'cause it's hard for Josh to get in a car, but the van's big and you can put his whole wheelchair in it, but ya gotta buckle his chair in so he don't go rollin' all over. We was gonna take you, but your door was closed."

From his expression, Anna could see that Liam realized that Colm was not happy when the door was closed. "It was nice that you wanted to ask me, but I have to work. Just like you have to work. Only I work here—"

"And I work at the store. Yeah, I know. And I get to work with lots of friends like Vic and Ariel. You gotta work all by yourself." Colm hurried over and hugged Liam. "Sorry, Liam. If you wanna come to work with me sometime, you can. I don't got no door, so I won't even close it."

Liam laughed. "Maybe someday I'll bring my computer to the cafeteria and work there while you work in the store."

"Oh, yeah, we could ride the bus together. That'd be fun."

Anna had ridden the bus with Colm and knew that he was very much at home on his route now. He knew all the bus drivers by name and a lot of the passengers, too. "Colm, you were telling Liam about the beach."

"Oh, yeah. It was lotsa fun. Anna, she pushed Josh on this ramp thing, 'cause it's hard to push wheelchairs in the sand. Only this guy there, he said they make special chairs with big wheels and maybe next time we'll get one of those for Josh so he can come closer to the water with me and Gilly. But today, Anna pushed him on the wooden thing and me and Gilly, we picked up glass and rocks. We made Josh hold the bucket, 'cause even if his hands don't work so good, he can hold buckets. We're gonna take all our beach rocks and put 'em in the garden when we get a house."

Anna almost groaned. She wanted to be the

first to tell Liam that. "Liam," she started. Immediately, she could see a flash of anger in his eyes.

Colm dug in his pocket. "And here, I got this cool one for you, Liam."

He handed it to Liam. Liam took it absent-mindedly. He continued staring at Anna.

Anna didn't want Liam to think this was her avoiding telling him something. "Liam, I can explain."

"So, what about this house, Colm?" Liam asked instead.

Colm was oblivious to the tension. "Gilly and Josh're gonna get a house together and said maybe I could move in, too, 'cause the three of us is best friends. Anna's bought them a house, only some people don't want Gilly 'n Josh to move in, but Anna's gonna fight 'em, and then they'll build some ramps for Josh, and they'll move in, and maybe me, too. I'd sure like to have my own house with the guys. You used to have your own house, Liam, 'fore Mommy and Daddy went to heaven and you moved in here."

Liam was furious. It took no special ability to see it. "Liam, I—"

He interrupted her. "Colm, why don't you get washed up for supper? Do you think you can set the table for me afterwards?"

"For us and Anna?"

"Uh, I don't think I'm staying tonight, Colm," Anna said.

"Okay," he said, agreeable. "I'll set the table real good, Liam. Bye, Anna."

"Bye, Colm."

He ran out of the kitchen and Anna could hear him running up the stairs.

"Let's take this to the porch," Liam said, his voice raw.

They went outside and Anna remembered the first day she'd arrived, how much she'd loved this porch. Right now, she'd rather be anywhere but here. "So, this is another one of your spring-it-on-Liam tricks? I never wanted this. I don't want Colm to move out. I never wanted Colm to get a job. You've pushed and prodded, forcing us to do what you think is for the best. I came to you in order to get some help for my brother, now you're moving him into a group home without even consulting me?"

"Liam, that's not it." She tried to explain,

but his expression said he wasn't buying it. "Of course not. I was going to try and talk to you the other day, but then you kissed me and I lost all track of my thoughts. I was going to talk to you tonight. I—"

He shook his head. "I think this is all a mistake."

"Liam!" She didn't have to ask if by all this he meant her working with Colm as well as their budding relationship.

"I think you'd better go. And I don't think you should come back." Liam's tone was flat, as if devoid of emotion. But his face revealed what his tone didn't. He felt betrayed and there was no way to hide that kind of hurt.

"Liam, really, please let me explain." She didn't want things to end like this. She'd grown to love Colm…and Liam, she admitted to herself. She'd never told him that and suddenly she wished she had, because given the way he was acting now, she was never going to get another chance. "Please, give me a minute to—"

"No. Your time's up. I don't want to hear any explanation, Anna. I don't want you to tell me how I've messed up with Colm—how my parents messed up with him. We—"

"I've never said that. I've never even thought that."

"Colm and I were fine before you came along."

He could be furious with her, and he could kick her out, but she wasn't going to let that particular lie stand. She'd promised herself she wouldn't allow her relationship with Liam to interfere with her doing what was best for Colm. So she said the words that needed to be said, even though she knew they'd hurt him more. "You were fine, Liam. Colm wasn't. He was stagnating. You loved him and he knew that—knows that. But he was and is capable of so much more than you gave him credit for. He—"

"Just go."

Anna's heart was breaking. She should have shut up. Ceelie would say that sometimes her heart ran away from her brain, and she'd be right. "May I say goodbye to Colm?"

Liam shook his head. "I don't think that would be wise."

"Liam, I don't understand why it feels like

everything about Colm is a battle for us. I know you love him and that you want what's best for him. I don't see how you think keeping him dependent and isolated is what's best for either of you."

He gritted the words through his clenched jaw. "You really think that's what I'm doing?"

Anna wanted to reach out and take his hand in hers, conversely, she wanted to shake him. She didn't get his attitude. Try as she might, she just didn't get it. "Yes. What would you call it?"

"I'd call it taking care of my brother. Looking out for him. You waltz in here and after what—three months?—you think you know what's best for him? I've been with Colm his entire life. You're going to have to trust me." He paused. "No, actually you don't, because I'm pulling Colm from Sunrise. Like I said, it's time for you to leave and let things around here get back to normal."

"I wasn't going to spring anything on you," Anna said quietly. "I was assessing how well Colm fit in with Gilly and Josh and thought maybe we'd talk about the possibility of him going into a supervised group home eventually. I never said a word. Gilly did. He and Gilly have gotten very close."

Her words weren't having any impact.

"Good luck then, Liam. I hope you know what you're doing, but I don't think you do. You're a wonderful man. A man I thought I was falling for, but I was wrong. Because there's something there. Something festering in you. These moments of anger that I don't understand. I've watched my mother try to change the men she falls for, and I won't make that mistake. I know I can't change you, just like you can't change me. And I also know that in your heart you want what's best for Colm. I hope you figure that out, Liam, I really do, because right now I don't think you have a clue."

She turned and walked to her car trying to hold back the tears. They would come. She was sure they would come. But she'd do her darndest to see that they didn't come until she was away from here.

She glanced back at Liam, standing on the porch.

So angry.

So alone.

She kept holding back the tears and went, knowing she was leaving a big part of her heart there with both of the Franklin brothers.

LIAM STAYED on the porch after Anna had pulled away. Her car had barely rounded the corner when he came to the realization that he was a bona fide ass.

"Liam! Anna!" Colm called from inside.

"I'm out here, bud," he called back.

Colm burst through the door. "Hey, Anna—" He stopped. "Where's Anna?"

"Uh, she had to go."

"That's okay. I'll give her my picture tomorrow. I made a bunch, but this is my favorite. I made it for that wall at her work. Is she coming tomorrow?" He held the painting out to Liam.

Liam studied it. He could make out a lot. In the middle there was a bus with a smiling circle for the driver. In the upper-right corner was a rectangle he assumed was Keller's Market. There were a bunch of smiling, stick figureish people standing outside, holding hands. In the bottom-left corner was their house and four people in front of it. Three were smiling, and one was frowning. "Who are they?" Liam asked, pointing.

"That's me. That's Anna. That's Aunt Betty. And that's you."

Liam was the frowning stick figure.

"Will Anna be here tomorrow? I wanna give her the picture. It's the best."

"No, I don't think so." Liam studied Colm's efforts. Everyone was smiling and happy in the painting. Everyone but him.

"Okay, the next day then. That Anna, she sure is busy, Liam. She helps me and Gilly and Josh, and there're other people, too. Anna's sad about the house thing and me and Gilly and Josh wanna help her, but we don't know how. Do you?"

"No, I don't, Colm. I don't know much of anything right now."

Colm patted his back. "Aw, that's all right, don't worry 'cause you don't know, 'cause Anna says nobody knows everythin'. When me, Josh and Gilly move in we'll help those people and they'll figure out we're nice and like us."

"Colm, you won't be moving into the

house, bud. You've got a house here with me, remember?"

Colm frowned. The expression looked foreign on his face. "Yeah, Liam, but you had your own house 'til Mommy and Daddy…" He didn't say the word *died*. He let the sentence hang there. "You moved in to take care of me, but I can take care of myself. Gilly says that after we move in the house, Anna'll still come help us learn to do stuff. And you can come to supper. I'll cook spaghetti, 'cause I'm good at that, and Josh and Gilly'll help, but you won't 'cause you'll be our guest. And then we'll get dessert and maybe play some Go Fish. I wonder if Gilly and Josh know that game?"

"Colm, you're not going to move in with Gilly and Josh," Liam said more forcefully. "I'm sorry if Anna told you differently, but you're not moving. You live here, with me."

"Anna didn' say nothin'. But Gilly said—"

"I can't help what Gilly said. You live here." Liam tried not to think about the fact that Colm had admitted that it wasn't Anna, but rather Gilly who'd brought up the idea of Colm moving into the group home.

Colm was no longer frowning. He was glaring at Liam. "You'll see, Liam. I'll ask Anna, and she'll help me get ready to move."

"I don't think Anna's coming back." Liam figured he would be relieved, but the thought of not seeing Anna hurt.

"Why? Did I do somethin'?" Colm's anger had faded, and he sounded nervous and unsure of himself.

"No, bud, it wasn't anything you did," Liam assured him. "Anna's not coming back because we don't need her. It's you and me, like it used to be."

"I don't want that. Not like it used to be. I don't wanna sit here in the house by myself watchin' the stupid TV. I want my job, and I want my friends. I want Anna to come teach me stuff, 'cause she thinks I'm smart. You just think I'm dumb but I'm not."

"I don't think that, Colm. I think you need help with some things."

"That's what Anna says, 'You just need some help, Colm.' But I don't need help from you. I want Anna." He stormed into the house and slammed the door.

Liam followed on his heels. "Colm,

everyone needs help sometimes. I will help you."

"No. I can do stuff by myself, Liam. I don't want you to do it for me."

"Colm—"

Colm ignored Liam and walked away, starting up the stairs. He stopped and turned around. "And I want Anna to teach me more, Liam."

"We'll talk about it later, bud," Liam said tiredly. He was exhausted. Bone-deep exhausted.

He was tired of being angry. Tired of feeling as if he'd let everyone down. Colm. Anna.

"No, not later." Colm came back down the stairs. "I can learn, and Anna teaches me. I don't want to talk, I want her to teach me."

He turned, stomped up the stairs, and slammed his bedroom door.

After years of being easygoing, Colm was asserting himself. Fighting for what he wanted.

Thanks to Anna, Liam thought angrily.

He walked back out to the front porch and sat down.

Slowly, the anger that had coiled up in his stomach began to burn less hotly.

Colm had said that Anna hadn't said anything about him moving out. His friend Gilly had. So, Liam's accusations were off. He'd been wrong. And he hadn't listened when she'd tried to explain.

He should probably call and apologize. He could tell she'd been about to cry when she left.

Liam's emotions were a mess. He was relieved that Anna was gone and things could get back to normal. And yet, he'd miss her. He missed her already. It was almost a physical ache. And he was angry. Still so damned angry. That, at least, was familiar. Liam couldn't remember a time when he hadn't been angry. The feeling was an old friend. He was comfortable with it.

For a while, he'd thought it was gone for good, but he should have known better.

THE NEXT MORNING, Anna arrived at Sunrise at seven-thirty to do some paperwork before going out on her day's appointments. That was her story in case Ceelie showed up early. In actuality, Anna hadn't been able to sleep and had finally decided that if she wasn't sleeping she might as well be working.

Finding a parking space on Main Street was frequently a challenge, but it turned out that at seven-thirty, there were plenty. She collected her things and hurried to the door…and found Colm.

"Hi, Anna." He grinned and clutched a rolled-up piece of paper to his chest.

Anna looked up and down the block, but didn't see anyone else. "Colm, where's Liam?"

"At home. In bed. He stayed up really late last night watchin' TV. He wouldn't let me stay up. No, he said, 'Colm, go to bed, bud.'"

Anna unlocked Sunrise's door and beckoned Colm inside. "How did you get here?"

"I rode the bus."

"Does Liam know?"

"Nah, he was still sleeping, so I got dressed and made my breakfast, then waited for a bus. I waited a real long time."

Anna wondered how early Colm had started his journey. "Come on back to my office. We'd better call Liam. He'll be worried if he wakes up and finds you gone."

The last person in the world she wanted to talk to today was Liam Franklin, especially since she was running on a couple of hours of sporadic sleep herself. She didn't feel capable of holding her own if they had another fight, but it didn't appear she had a choice. "Come on."

Colm shook his head and held his ground, his arms folded across his chest. "No, Anna. I don't wanta. He's just gonna say, 'No, Colm, you go sit in your room and watch TV.' Well, I don't wanna go sit in my room. I wanna have you teach me more stuff. I want my job. I wanna live with Josh and Gilly at the house."

Anna could hear the frustration in his voice. She could see it quivering in his tightly clenched fists. She didn't know how to help him. "Colm," she started.

"No, Anna. I won't do it. I'm not some little kid. I'm not real smart, like Liam, but I can learn stuff and do stuff and I wanna."

She reached out and gently touched his arm. "I know."

Colm jerked away from her touch. "And that Liam, he can't make me not do 'em. He can't make me stay home. I'm not a kid."

"Well, Colm, you're sort of acting like a little kid now, not a grown-up," Anna tenderly pointed out.

That stopped him. "Huh?"

"Grown-ups don't run away from their troubles. They talk to the other person. They make them understand what's important."

"You ran away."

"I didn't." Liam had kicked her out. She wasn't going to say that to Colm, but he had and it wasn't the same thing.

"Yeah, you did. You don't talk to Liam and make him understand."

Maybe she should have tried harder. Maybe she should have talked to him earlier about Colm moving into the house with Josh and Gilly. But she'd wanted to be sure— well, as sure as she could be—that it would be the right thing for Colm, and for Josh and Gilly before she discussed it with Liam. She wanted to feel confident that the three of them meshed and were capable of handling a house. She should have said all that, even if she had to force him to listen. "You're right. I should have stayed and tried to make him understand. We both should have."

Colm sighed. "Yeah, 'cause we ain't kids. We're grown-ups and grown-ups don't run away."

"Looks like we've got a bit of a mess on our hands. Any suggestions?"

Colm nodded. "Yep. When you make a mess you clean it up."

"That's right. So, let's head back to your house and clean things up." She wasn't going to call. She was going to go over and make Liam listen. And she was going to hope he'd talk to her, explain things to her. He could be the most wonderful man in the world, but when it came to Colm, he was fiercely resistant to change.

"Hey, Anna, I brought you this, for your wall." Colm thrust the paper at her.

Anna studied it. Keller's Market, the house. "You, me, Aunt Betty and Liam?" she asked, pointing to the four stick figures.

"Yeah, that Liam, he's all mad again."

"You know he's not mad at you, right?" she said.

Colm didn't answer. Instead, he said, "Don't ever leave, Anna. I love you."

Anna hugged him. "I love you, too, Colm."

"And you've got lots more to teach me."

"Maybe. But you've taught me a lot, too." Like how to be open and honest…and not back down from a fight. Liam might not care about her the way she cared about him, but she knew he loved Colm and wanted what was best for him, even if doing what was best was hard.

"Come on, let's go."

CHAPTER TEN

LIAM AWOKE to the sound of someone alternately banging on the front door and ringing the bell, then there was silence.

He glanced at the clock. It wasn't even eight yet. Aunt Betty wasn't supposed to be coming today.

Trying not to think about how little sleep he'd actually managed last night, he stumbled out of bed and headed down to the front door. There was a more polite single ring of the bell as he reached the bottom step. He opened the door and found Anna and Colm there.

"Anna?"

She looked guarded as she explained, "I got to Sunrise this morning and Colm was waiting for me. He rode the bus."

"You left the house without telling me?" Liam asked, only his asking came out more like yelling. Rather than looking cowed, Colm glared at him.

"Yeah, 'cause I ain't a kid. You can't say, 'No more Anna, Colm.' You can't make me stay home and watch the stupid TV. I wanna work and I want Anna to teach me. Anna wants me to learn stuff, not like you."

Liam wasn't sure how he'd made such a mess of things. Anna, who normally was an open book, was closed and wary. Colm, who was normally the happiest, most easygoing person ever, was furious. "Colm, of course I want you to learn things."

"Nah, you want me here in this stupid house. I was gonna run away and live with Anna 'til my new house with Gilly and Josh was ready, but I ain't a kid. I'm a grown-up and I don't run away." He walked past Liam and started up the stairs then turned around and shouted, "And I ain't gonna listen to you, Liam. You're just my brother. I'm gonna go to work and see Anna. And you can't stop me." He turned and stomped up the stairs, down the hall and slammed the door shut.

Liam sighed. "I've never seen Colm like this. He's never had a temper tantrum before."

Anna shook her head. "That wasn't a temper tantrum, that was an adult asserting himself. Colm's had a taste of what he can do, and he likes it. I don't see anything wrong with that."

"I don't agree. I'm afraid he's going to be hurt."

"So you've said. Everyone gets hurt sometimes, Liam. I can't promise you that he won't be. But that's no reason to keep him shut away. He's right. You're wrong."

"I know I was wrong about the way I talked to you yesterday, accusing you of telling Colm he could move out. I was going to call you later and ask you to come back."

"Back to working with Colm. To what end? I don't want to fight, Liam, but really, if I did come back and work with Colm, what good will that do if all you do is fight to keep the status quo? All it does is hurt him when he learns he can do and be more, only to discover you don't want that for him."

"That's not it, Anna. That's not fair." Liam didn't know how to explain his feelings to her when he didn't understand them himself. "I want Colm to go however far he wants."

"Do you mean that?"

He could see the doubt in her eyes and he hated that he was the one to put it there. "I don't like it, but I do mean it. Although I'm not sure about him moving out. And I don't like the fact he got picked on at work. Anna, I'm so confused. I don't know what to do, what's right for him. Give me some time."

"Fine. Then consider me back. Tell Colm I'll be here tomorrow, the way we originally scheduled." She started back toward her car.

"Anna, wait," Liam called. "About us..."

For a moment, he thought she was going to keep walking, as if she hadn't heard him. In the end she turned around, and he almost wished she hadn't. He could see the pain in her face. "Don't worry, there is no us, Liam."

"What if I want there to be?"

She shook her head. "I'm sorry. I can't do it again."

He'd known yesterday he was ruining things, but he hadn't been able to stop himself. "Listen, I'm sorry. I don't understand why it bothers me, but it does. I just take time to adjust. I messed up, but—"

Anna walked over to him and took his

hand. "Liam, this is truly a case of it's not you, it's me." She searched for some way to explain. She noticed the two battered lawn chairs nearby. "It's like your porch."

Liam wasn't sure he'd understood her correctly. "My porch?"

"Yeah. Remember when I told you I had porch envy the first time I was here?"

Despite everything, he smiled at the memory. "Yes."

"Okay, so I want a porch, and yours is nice for the short term. I mean, to sit out here for a bit and watch the neighborhood go by is nice, but the chairs aren't really comfortable. They're not meant for long-term use. They're something that you fold up and put away when you're done with them. When I get my own porch, the porch I'm going to keep forever, I want one that's comfortable. That won't become uncomfortable and leave me fidgeting…"

He finally got her analogy. "You want white wicker."

She nodded. "Yes."

"And all I have to offer you is ratty lawn chairs." He hated that it was so, but he knew the truth of it—he was a ratty lawn chair, and someone like Anna deserved white wicker.

"Liam, I've told you about my mom and her never-ending search for the right man. For her one true love. I've seen her work at relationships. I've seen her try to change for them. I've watched her try to change the other person. Neither way works. I decided a long time ago that I'm not worried about ever-after. I don't want to change you, and I won't change myself for you. I think it's best to admit we're not meant for anything more than what this was—a brief fling."

"And you want white wicker."

"Yes."

Liam had no argument. Anna Chapel thought all she wanted was a relationship that was comfortable for however long she was in it. She said she didn't believe in soul mates. But Liam knew that Anna deserved nothing less than a partner who could love her heart and soul. That's the type of relationship she was meant to have, and even if she wasn't looking for it, he knew she'd get it someday. She was too special not to.

And because he understood all that, even

if she didn't, he didn't argue. He simply said, "Fine. But you'll come back for Colm?"

"Yes." She started for her car again, then turned around and said, "About…well, I'm sorry."

"So am I, Anna."

Liam was pretty sure he wasn't going to get over being sorry anytime soon…he wasn't sure he ever would.

Liam dragged himself upstairs and knocked on Colm's door. "May I come in?"

"Yeah." Colm was sitting on his bed. Liam looked around the room and realized that very little had ever changed in here. Colm's collection of Star Wars figures and toys lined the bookshelf. Crates of Lego were tucked under the bed. Looking at the room it would be easy to believe that Colm was still a child.

But looking at his brother, Liam knew he wasn't.

Colm's face mirrored Liam's own, only happier. More innocent.

He remembered the picture Colm had been working on. The one where everyone was smiling except himself.

Is that how Colm saw him? How everyone saw him?

"Colm, we have to talk."

"Yeah, 'cause we're both grown-ups and grown-ups don't run away from stuff. They talk about it."

"Anna said that?"

Colm nodded. "And that grown-ups fight for what they want. I want Anna to teach me."

"She said to tell you she'll be on time tomorrow."

Colm threw himself at Liam and hugged him. "Thanks, Liam. Anna was right. Anna's always right."

Anna who'd told him he was a ratty lawn chair was always right. Liam flopped onto the end of Colm's bed.

"Liam, how come you're mad at Anna?" Colm asked.

"I'm not," he assured Colm.

"Then she's mad at you?"

"No."

Colm patted Liam's shoulder. "You're sad again. Your eyes crinkle and here, too," he said pointing at Liam's brow. "You're sad or mad a lot."

"I'm not mad right now, bud. I'm sad that I screwed up. I liked Anna. A lot."

"Anna says if you make a mistake you gotta clean it up." Colm studied him. "Yeah, you're sad 'bout Anna, but you're mad, too."

Before he thought about it, Liam said, "I'm mad that I'm the brother who got everything."

Liam heard the words come out of his mouth, but it was as if someone else had said them. Where had that come from?

Colm looked as confused as Liam felt. "Huh?"

Liam tried to explain, as much for himself as for Colm. "When we were born, I came first, but it took a long time, and you were stuck in Mommy's belly and didn't get enough air, so you didn't come out soon enough. You didn't get enough air and…" Liam stopped, unable to believe he'd said that. He'd never said those words aloud, but he realized that was exactly how he felt. Angry that he and Colm were twins. Identical twins. That Colm could have had all the things Liam did, if it wasn't for an accident at birth. If he hadn't been the second twin to be born.

Colm didn't seem distressed by Liam's admission. He simply nodded his head. "Oh, yeah, Mommy told me that. I didn't get 'nuf air, so it's harder for me to do some things."

"Yes."

Colm looked puzzled. "And you feel mad at me?"

"No, not at you. Never at you. I'm mad that that's how it worked out—I was the lucky brother." And there it was, the heart of his anger. He was the lucky brother—he'd gotten it all. And Colm, his identical twin, because he happened to be born second, had lost out. Liam knew he owed it to his brother to look after him, to somehow try to make up for the fact that Liam was the lucky twin.

Colm laughed. "Geesh, Liam, you were a baby. And it might take me longer to figure stuff out, but I do figure it out. And I got me a job, and I'm gonna get me a house with Gilly and Josh. And Anna's not mad at me. So, I'm really the lucky one, huh?"

Liam hadn't said yes to the house, hadn't agreed, but Colm didn't seem to realize that. He was making plans for his life. Plans he didn't consult Liam about. He was building his own future, as any adult would. "Colm…"

"Yep, I'm lucky 'cause you're gonna be all alone in the house when I go, and if Anna's mad, she won't even come over to visit you. She'll come see me and Gilly and Josh, though. If we get the house. Some of the people there don't want us."

"Anna will make sure you get the house. And if not that one, she'll find you another one." Anna would fight for what she believed in. She'd fight for Colm. For his friends. For their right to have the house. But she wasn't going to fight for him. Or rather, she had fought with him and for him and finally given up.

Colm nodded. "Yeah, 'cause Anna likes me."

"Yes, she does."

"And even if I'm the lucky brother and she likes me, she likes you, too. You gotta wipe up the mess. Say you're sorry."

"You think?" Liam asked.

"I know, you could make her a picture for her wall at work. I made her one and she liked it. It was a very nice picture. Since she's mad, you gotta paint her a really nice one and say you're sorry and maybe she won't be mad no more."

Suddenly, he had an idea. "Colm, you're

right. I've got to paint her something special. Something more special than a picture. Will you help me?" It was the first time he could ever remember asking his brother that question. It felt as though for the first time ever he was truly seeing Colm.

He wasn't seeing Colm's handicap. He was seeing his brother. An amazingly upbeat man who had dreams, aspirations, and who felt more joy than Liam had ever allowed himself to feel. And maybe that's why, for the first time, he asked Colm for help.

Colm articulated what Liam was thinking. "Yeah, I'll always help you, Liam, 'cause you're my brother. And you'll always help me, 'cause I'm your brother. That's what brothers do. They help each other."

"Yes, that's what brothers do." Liam threw his arms around his brother and hugged.

"Liam, you're squishing me," Colm said, laughter in his voice.

Liam released him and Colm reached over and patted his shoulder. "And you can't feel bad, Liam, 'cause I came second. Right now I'm the lucky brother. And I got friends and a job and I'll have a house soon. I'm real lucky."

"And happy?" Liam asked.

"Oh, yeah, real happy." He looked at Liam. "You're not happy though."

"Maybe I can be if Anna stops being mad at me." Liam knew there was no maybe about it. If Anna gave him another chance, he'd be the happiest man around. "So, let's get painting."

"What're we paintin'?" Colm asked.

"Come on and I'll show you. But first, we've got some shopping to do. And then, we've got a lot of work."

"Okay. Anna marked my work days on the calendar and I don't gotta go today. I gotta work at the grocery store tomorrow."

"Great. This might take all day."

It was seven o'clock before Liam was ready. He and Colm had taken a quick lunch break, then eaten pizza about five.

All day, every few minutes Colm had said, "Can we go get her now?"

And Liam had to say, "Not yet, bud, but soon."

Though, as Liam surveyed their day's work, he knew it was all ready. "Colm, it looks great. I couldn't have done it without you." And he couldn't have. "We make a good team."

"Yeah. So, let's go get Anna and show her her surprise."

Liam wiped his hands on his paint-splattered jeans. "Let's go." He started toward the car, but Colm wasn't at his side. He turned around and asked, "Problem?"

"You wanna take me to Aunt Betty's so you can get her yourself? You gotta say you're sorry, and then maybe you can kiss her again." Colm giggled, as if Liam and Anna kissing was one of the funniest things he'd ever heard of.

Liam laughed as well. He was nervous that he'd done irreparable damage to his relationship with Anna, but he had this underlying feeling of hope—that somehow he could make things right with her. "Nah, I think Anna might be more willing to come see our surprise if you're with me."

"Okay, but hey, if I'm there, no kissin' in front of me," Colm warned. "'Cause that's gross."

Liam laughed. Not because of Colm's proclamation about the grossness of his kissing Anna, but because he felt…happy. And optimistic. About a lot of things.

The weight of guilt was gone.

While he'd always know that Colm's handicap wasn't his fault, emotions don't always pay attention to such logic. But Colm's honest reasoning helped.

His brother was happy. He was living life on his own terms.

It was okay if Liam was happy, too.

And the only thing Liam needed to find that happiness was Anna Chapel.

"OH, ANNA, you'll never believe my news," her mother called out as she waltzed into Anna's without knocking.

Anna should yell. She should have the boundary discussion with her mom…again. But she couldn't muster the energy it required.

"Anna, why on earth are you sitting here in the dark?"

Anna was curled up on a corner of the couch. She thought about getting up, but couldn't quite muster the action. "It's not dark, Mom. It's still daylight out."

"Well, this room is positively gloomy. Turn on a light."

"I'm being green and trying to do my part

to save the planet," Anna stated. She didn't want her mother to see that she'd been crying. She didn't want to answer questions.

"Listen, I want to see my daughter's face when I tell her the good news."

Anna flipped on the light. Her mother was practically beaming. "What news, Mom?"

"I've met someone," she declared, as if she'd never said those words before. As if she'd never thought she'd found her soul mate in the past.

"Great." Anna tried to infuse the word with some enthusiasm, but feared she'd fallen short.

Her mother didn't seem to notice. "Not just anyone, but I've met *him*. The man I've been waiting for all these years. I know I've said that before. I can tell by your expression you're thinking that. And I have. But this time, it's different. He's different."

"I'm sure he is, Mom," Anna agreed. She had no fight left in her.

"No, Anna, I need you to understand. He's *different*." Her mother hugged herself with delight. "Every man I've been with since your father wasn't right for me, or I wasn't right for him. Every relationship was really about me trying to change him, or him trying to change me. I know this one is different because I don't need to change a thing about him. I wouldn't if I could. He's one of the worst dressers I've ever met. He thinks that plaid is a viable choice for…well, anything. But he loves me the way that I am. He said he waited his whole life to find me, why would he want to change anything?" She sighed a happy sigh. "I know you don't believe me, and I know I've given you reasons not to, but he's different. You'll see."

"I'm happy for you, Mom."

"You're not really happy though, are you, Anna Banana?" Her mother reached out and gently touched Anna's cheek, lightly tracing the path of her tears with her finger.

"I am," Anna lied.

"No. I know this look. I've lived this look too many times. You've got man trouble."

"No. I don't have a man, so how could I have trouble?"

"Ah." Her mother nodded as if she understood. "It's the don't-have part that is the problem, because from the look of you, you might not have, but you want to have."

"No."

"Anna, I know you've always prided yourself on thinking things through rather than simply feeling your way. I'm to blame for that, I know. I run in heart-first and I think later. And I've loved you enough to let you delude yourself into thinking you're different than me. But you're not. You like to believe you think first, feel later, but sweetie, you're all heart. And from the looks of you, your heart's hurting."

Before Anna could think of a rebuttal, someone knocked on the front door. All she wanted was to sit and mull, and suddenly she was being bombarded by people.

"You sit there, Anna. I'll get it." Her mom hurried out and Anna heard the door open and then her mom said, "Oh, she's going to be so glad to see you. She's got a broken heart and I'm not having any luck jollying her out of it."

"Anna?" Ceelie took one look at her and sighed. "I told you this wasn't going to end well."

"I don't know what you're talking about," Anna said.

"Liam," Ceelie replied.

Anna could see her mother latch on to her friend's comment. "Liam? That's a good strong name."

"He's a client's guardian," Ceelie supplied.

"Oh, Anna, you fell in love with Liam," her mother purred.

"I wasn't in love with Liam." And that was officially the biggest lie she'd ever told. And from her mother and Ceelie's expressions, they didn't believe her any more than she believed herself. "I—"

The doorbell rang again.

"I'll—" her mom started, but Anna interrupted.

"I'll get it."

Who else could it be? The newspaper boy collecting? Someone doing a survey? It didn't matter. Whoever was there was simply part of the cosmic plan to keep her from moping.

She was pretty sure the cosmos underestimated her moping skills because whoever it was didn't stand a chance of distracting her.

She opened the door. "Hello?"

Colm was grinning beneath the porch light. "Anna. It's me, Colm."

"Colm, what are you doing here at this time of night? I thought we agreed, no more running away from home."

"I didn't run away." Colm pointed at the car.

She looked past Colm and spotted Liam sitting in his car, his window down. "Hey, Anna."

She didn't respond to Liam, but instead asked Colm, "Why are you both here?"

"We came to kidnap you, Anna. We've got a surprise." Colm laughed with glee.

"And you're going to kidnap me for the surprise?"

"Yep. Me and Liam, we've got this big surprise and it can't wait 'til tomorrow, so you gotta come now."

Liam nodded. "Colm's right. We're hoping you have time to come with us for a surprise."

"Who is it, Anna?" her mother called.

Anna turned around and saw her mom and Ceelie standing in the doorway.

"It's Colm," she said.

"I thought she loved Liam?" her mom said to Ceelie.

"Colm is Anna's client and Liam's brother," Ceelie supplied.

"Oh." Her mom scanned beyond Anna and Colm, and spied Liam in the car. "Ohhh," she said again, dragging the word out longer this time and smiling.

"And I'm kidnappin' Anna for a surprise," Colm called out. "Me and Liam, we worked all day. It was hard work, Anna. But Liam, he needed my help. And you say it's okay to ask for help."

Anna smiled despite her mood. "Yes, I do. So you guys made up?"

"Yeah. Liam he thought he was the lucky brother 'cause he was born first so he was smarter. But I told him I was sorry, 'cause I was lucky. I got a job, I got friends, I got you. He's not very happy. But he will be when you see the surprise, so come on. You're kidnapped."

He took her hand. With her free hand, Anna snagged her keys from the table by the door and hollered, "Looks like I gotta go. Could you guys lock up when you leave?"

She didn't wait for a response. Couldn't. Colm was pulling her toward the car. He stopped at the passenger door where Liam was waiting.

"Here, Anna." Colm thrust a large piece of cloth at her. "You gotta put this on your eyes. No peeking."

"I have to be blindfolded?" she asked.

"Yep," Colm chirruped.

"Sorry," Liam said. He sounded…different. "Those are the rules."

Anna couldn't quite identify what the difference was, but it was there.

"Fine." She put the cloth over her eyes and tried to tie it behind her head, but it was an awkward position.

"Here, let me help." Liam's fingers brushed hers as he took the ends and tied them.

They helped her into Liam's car and drove a few minutes. As she sat, eyes blindfolded, she thought about Colm's words. Liam had thought he was the lucky brother. He'd felt guilty. Guilt. That could explain so much.

She'd dealt with parents who felt guilty about a child's condition, but it had never occurred to her that a brother—an identical twin brother—would feel it. Though she could tell Liam that his guilt didn't make sense, she knew that what the head might understand the heart didn't always feel.

She'd known that getting involved with Liam was a mistake, but she'd felt…

Sitting in the backseat of the car, blindfolded, she admitted, if only to herself, she'd felt love. She loved Liam.

The car stopped.

Car doors opened and shut. "Come on, Anna. No peeking." Colm took her hand and helped her out of the car.

"Watch yourself, there's a crack in the sidewalk," Liam said as she followed Colm forward.

He'd call and warn her, but he wouldn't touch her.

She took maybe a dozen steps and Colm stopped. "You ready?"

"Yes."

He had trouble with the blindfold.

Liam said, "Let me, bud."

Anna resisted the urge to lean into his touch. She had to find a way to get over Liam Franklin.

Moments later, she could see. But as her eyes adjusted, she wondered where she was for a split second, then she recognized Colm and Liam's house. Only it was different. The house was ablaze with light from both inside and outside the home.

The porch had been painted a bright kelly green. She looked up and could see he'd added shutters to all the front windows that were the same merry color.

But it wasn't the paint that really caught her attention. It was the wicker furniture. White wicker, with overstuffed floral cushions. There was a wicker coffee table and there were end tables, and at the end of the porch, there was a porch swing.

This was the porch of her dreams.

"Liam, Colm—" she started.

Liam interrupted. "I need you to hear me out. I know I don't deserve it, but I'm asking."

Anna nodded.

"It's my fault Colm is the way he is. We're twins. Identical twins. I was the first twin born. It took so much longer for Colm, and when he was born, his umbilical cord had been wrapped around his neck and compressed. He was deprived of oxygen. That's why he's…"

"Special," Colm supplied. "I'm special different, right, Anna?"

Anna nodded. "Right, Colm."

Liam continued. "Anna, I grew up knowing that it was my job to take care of him."

"Colm can take care of himself."

"I know. Well, I didn't know until you came into our lives, but the more independent he got, the more angry I became. I knew I should have been happy for him. And I know I was a pain in your, er…butt. It's only that I didn't understand what his growing independence would mean for me. I've always looked after Colm. I knew I owed him that and so much more."

"Liam, it never was your fault," Anna said.

"I've been angry for so many years. Angry at the things I could do and Colm couldn't. Angry that he had to deal with a world that was frequently unkind. Just angry. And suddenly you were here, and Colm was…well, growing up."

"And you were angry."

"Yeah, but Liam, he wasn't mad at me or you," Colm said, trying to reassure Anna. She took his hand and gave it a squeeze.

"Anger is so much easier to deal with than guilt," Liam admitted. "I've been angry at fate my whole life. And with Colm learning to live life on his own terms, I didn't know what to do with all that anger. I didn't know how to live my own life. I wasn't simply angry anymore, I was scared and that made me more angry. But now…"

"Now?" Anna pressed.

"I'm not angry anymore. Colm assured me in so many words that I do not need to look after my brother. He's capable of doing that himself. He also told me he feels bad for me because he's the lucky brother. He has a job he loves, friends…and he still had you, while I'd pushed you away."

"I wasn't planning to stay away."

"You weren't?"

She studied him, this gentle man who might not know it yet, but who was loved, too. "You should be aware by now that I'm more stubborn than that. I was hurt, but I'd have healed and I would have come back on my own."

"I'm glad I beat you to it this once." He gestured at the porch. "Anna, sometimes with some work, ratty lawn chairs can become white wicker. And before you argue that people shouldn't change for someone else, I'm not changing for you—I'm changing because of you. And because of my brother. For the first time in my life, I'm not feeling angry or guilty. I'm feeling grateful. Grateful that I have a brother who will help me when I need it, and grateful for you. I'm willing to do whatever I need to in order to win you back. I—"

He didn't finish the sentence because Anna had flung herself into his arms and was kissing him.

"Oh, gross," Colm exclaimed. "I told ya about the kissin', Liam. Wait 'til I tell Josh and Gilly you two were kissing. They'll say yuck, too."

Both Anna and Liam ignored Colm's gagging sounds. "I love you. I don't want you to be guilty or angry. I want you to be happy."

"I will be…if you're with me."

"Oh, no, don't do it. Don't kiss again," Colm yelled. "I painted all day and all this kissin' is awful."

Anna wasn't sure what painting all day and kissing had to do with each other, but she didn't care. She wasn't sure of much except for the fact she loved Liam Franklin, and, though he hadn't said the words, she knew he loved her, too. After all, he'd given her white wicker.

"Do you remember on our trip to Ferrante's when you asked me what my dream was?" Liam whispered in her ear.

Anna nodded.

"I never dreamed because I never felt I had the right to. But I found my dream in you, Anna. I can't think of any better dream than sitting on this front porch with you for the rest of my life."

EPILOGUE

"So, ARE WE ready?" Ceelie asked three months later.

It was a hot October evening, but Anna knew that the last of the year's heat had nothing to do with her sweat. She looked around City Council's chambers and tried not to be nervous. "As ready as we're ever going to be, I suppose. I wish I could make these folks see that having Sunrise clients as neighbors is a good thing."

The room was packed. Anna thought she and Ceelie were very much David versus the neighborhood Goliath. There had to be twenty or more people staring at them. She spotted her mom and Doug in the audience. They were still going strong. Anna had never seen her mother so happy, and if only for that she'd have liked Doug, but he was genuinely a very nice man.

A genuinely nice man who was wearing the most horrendous plaid shirt she'd ever seen. Not that her mother seemed to notice or care.

"I'm glad we didn't ask the boys to come. Josh would be terrified facing all these people," Anna said.

She and Ceelie had gone round and round about whether Colm, Gilly and Josh should be here. Maybe if the neighbors saw their potential new residents they wouldn't be so nervous. Ultimately, Anna had decided not to have them here. She didn't want to see them hurt.

"Still, maybe they could have swayed these people. Let them really see that they're not monsters."

"They shouldn't have to prove themselves like that," Anna said. "It's not fair."

Ceelie snorted. "You know what you'd say if a client said that? That life's not fair and—"

Anna was saved from hearing Ceelie throw her own words back at her as Liam walked into the Council Chambers.

She smiled. Ever since the "kidnapping," things had been good. Not perfect, but really, really good. Colm was thriving. He had a job he loved, and according to Zac Keller, he was great at it. And he had friends. If this house didn't work out, Anna would find another, because Colm, Josh and Gilly deserved a home of their own.

She spotted Colm behind Liam.

When they reached her, she shook her head. "You'd better take Colm home, Liam. He could hear things that might upset him. A lot."

"He wanted to be here." Liam kissed her cheek. And in that small gesture, she found comfort.

"Yeah, Anna," Colm said. "These guys ain't mad at you, they're mad at me and Josh and Gilly, so I thought maybe if I talked to 'em, they'd figure out we're only a little different."

Anna's heart clenched at the thought. "Colm, I don't know if they'll be respectful. They're sort of mad."

"It's okay, Anna. I'll tell 'em they don't need to be scared of us."

She turned to Liam for support, but rather than speaking up and telling Colm that he should sit down, Liam said, "I've learned that when my brother sets his mind to something, there's no stopping him. Anna, you've already talked to all the neighbors—countless times these last few months. You haven't been able to make them understand, but maybe hearing Colm will help change their minds."

Colm nodded. "Yeah, I wanna help, Anna."

"How?" she asked, not sure what they could do exactly.

Gilly came into the room, pushing Josh's wheelchair. "Hey, Anna. Here we are," he called loudly, focusing the entire room's attention on them as they walked up the aisle and joined the small group. Liam moved a folding chair to make room for Josh's wheelchair.

"Here we are, Colm. Me and Josh. It took a while to get Josh in. His chair buzzes the machine at the door so they had to check him. I didn't buzz," Gilly said.

Colm patted his friend on the back, then turned to Anna. "Let me talk to 'em. Me, Gilly and Josh. It's gonna be our house, so we should help."

Colm was determined. And like Liam, Anna had learned to appreciate that when Colm wanted to do something, there was no dissuading him.

"You're sure, Colm? There are a lot of people here. Neighbors who don't want the group home. The City Council members will be arriving any minute. You'll have to talk to all of them."

The coach in her was proud that Colm was ready to take this on, but as someone who loved him, she couldn't stand the thought of him being upset by the neighbors.

"That's okay, Anna. I can do this."

She sighed. "I know you can."

Colm took that as the matter being settled and started talking to Gilly about their house.

While they were distracted, Anna turned to Liam. "I don't want to see him hurt."

"A very wise person has convinced me that my brother is capable of more than I've ever given him credit for. Win or lose, he'll have accomplished something big simply by attempting to sway people. Remember those boys at the store? He dealt with them. He can do this." Liam kissed her forehead. "My brother is an amazing man."

"I'd say both Franklin brothers are amazing."

The five Council members took their seats at the long table at the front of the room. The meeting was called to order and a number of issues were discussed before they announced they'd be talking about the Trudy Street variance next.

Miriam Mark, this year's Council President, read the formal request for a variance, and the zoning board's positive response. "But we have some complaints from the neighbors. Council will hear your concerns now."

One by one, neighbors stood, talking about lowered property values and concerns about having handicapped people in the neighborhood. One woman in particular was adamant in her protest. "I've lived in this neighborhood for fifty years," Mrs. Albright said.

Anna had tried to talk to Mrs. Albright countless times in the last few months, but the woman had remained staunch in her disapproval, and was part of the driving force that had convinced the other neighbors to reject the variance.

"Families have come and gone in that house next door," Mrs. Albright said. "Families. That's the key. This is a family neighborhood. And none of us want that to change. If you give this variance, it will. And what if this group moves out of the home, will we have opened a window to something even further removed from the family ideal this neighborhood has always presented? Please, vote no to this variance. We don't want to see our neighborhood change."

She sat down, and all the neighbors clapped wildly.

Miriam banged her gavel. "And now, we'll hear from a representative of The Sunrise Foundation."

Anna got up and felt wobbly-kneed as she approached the microphone. "Hi. I'm Anna Chapel, and I'm here on behalf of The Sunrise Foundation. We're a small local organization founded to help meet the special needs of some members of our community. We're dedicated to helping exceptional people in Whedon, Pennsylvania—in all of George County, Pennsylvania—live exceptional lives. We have two other group homes, and I have to be clear that by *group homes* we're talking small groups of three or four individuals. Both of the homes receive supervision from Sunrise. But in essence, the residents are individuals who have come together to form a family. Whedon's zoning policy reads that no more than two unrelated adults can share a premises, and that's why when Sunrise buys a house, we need to apply for a variance. I've brought affidavits from the neighbors of our two other homes, testifying to the fact that our clients make great neighbors. I planned to talk about our program, but I've decided to turn the microphone over to someone who I think will say it better than I ever could. With your permission?" she asked the Council.

Miriam nodded. "Please."

Anna turned and beckoned Colm forward. "This is Colm Franklin, one of Sunrise's clients. He's also one of the men who hopes to live in the Trudy Street house." She moved over and gave him room at the mike.

"Hi, I'm Colm," he shouted into the microphone, practically blasting everyone from their seats.

Anna leaned over and whispered, "Inside voice," into his ear.

"Hi, I'm Colm," he said again, this time at a softer level. "And I'm a little different. It takes me longer to figure some stuff out, but I can figure it out. Anna's my friend and she helps me. I can ride the bus and go to the grocery store. I can cook. Sometimes it's not good, but Anna says sometimes her cookin's not good neither. Anna says everyone makes mistakes. If you make a mistake, you clean it up. Then you gotta try again. So, I try and sometimes it's good and sometimes not. But I got a job at Keller's Market, and I'm real good at packing the bags. I never put the bread or the eggs on the bottom 'cause they get smooshed. I didn't know that the first time, but Ariel at the store she told me that things that smoosh go on top. Maybe you didn't know somethin' the first time, too. I'm nice. And so are Gilly and Josh. They're gonna be my roommates." He paused and pointed to his friends in the audience.

Both men smiled and waved to the crowd.

"We don't have no loud parties, and we clean up real good 'cause Mr. Keller at the store won't let no one be messy there. We just want a house and we want to work. Anna says we're a little different, but that's not scary, that's special. She says different's not bad, it's just different. That's all I got to say."

Anna came back to the microphone and whispered in Colm's ear, "You did great."

He sat down next to Liam, Gilly and Josh.

She moved in front of the microphone again. "Colm's right. He's different, but he's very, very special. When I first met him, I thought I had a lot to teach him. He'd been coddled and waited on all his life and had never even poured himself a drink. But he learned how to do that and a lot of other things. Yet, in the end, he's taught me so much more than I've ever taught him. Colm and all my clients teach me on a daily basis about joy, about forgiveness, about hope. If you allow the neighbors to convince you to deny this variance, then you'll not only be denying three very special men a chance at the home they deserve, you'll be denying the neighborhood a chance to reap the benefits of having these three exceptional, caring men be a part of their lives. And they may never know it, but their lives will be so much the poorer for that."

She sat down.

Miriam stood. "Thank you, Ms. Chapel and Mr. Franklin. If that's it, the Council can vote now. Who says—"

"Wait," Mrs. Albright said, standing and

taking up the microphone again. "May I say one more thing?"

"Yes," Miriam said, sitting back down.

Mrs. Albright glanced back and Anna saw the older woman look directly at Colm a moment. Colm noticed as well, and rather than be disgruntled with the woman who'd spearheaded the move to keep him from moving into the Tracy Street house, he waved.

Mrs. Albright's expression softened, and she waved back before turning back to the microphone. "We've changed our minds."

Miriam pulled the microphone in front of her and said, "Pardon?"

"I think I speak for the entire neighborhood when I say we'd welcome Colm and his friends." She paused, glanced back at Colm again before continuing. "And I'm speaking strictly for myself when I stand here and apologize to the Council for taking up so much time, and to Colm, Josh and…" She hesitated.

"Gilly," Colm called out. "His name is Gilly. Really it's Gilbert, but he don't like that, so he's Gilly."

"And I apologize to Gilly. I'm old. I'll be eighty-two in a month. I used to tell myself that my body might be aging, but my mind was still sharp. Well, it may be sharp, but my mind's obviously forgotten something important—that different isn't something to be afraid of. Sometimes it's special. I'm a different woman than I was twenty, even ten years ago. My world has gotten progressively smaller, and it's become a scary place. Change frightens me. And I let my fear loose on my neighbors and convinced them this group home would be a detriment to the neighborhood. But after listening to Colm, I realize that this group home might be the best thing to happen to the neighborhood—to me—in a long time. So, please, may I retract what I said earlier?"

"You're sure, Mrs. Albright?"

Mrs. Albright looked back at Colm for a third time, and this time, she smiled. "Yes, I'm sure."

"Then, since there is no protest pending, it is my pleasure to grant the variance for the Trudy Street property. Colm, Josh and Gilly, it seems that you have a home."

Miriam adjourned the meeting, and soon Colm and his friends were surrounded by their new neighbors. Anna overheard Colm saying to Mrs. Albright, "Yeah, you're old. I help old people with their groceries at the store. I can help with yours. And me and Gilly'll help shovel snow and stuff, too. We're awfully strong."

Rather than take offense, Mrs. Albright laughed.

Anna cocked her head to one side and looked at Ceelie who read her mind. "You're not going to do it here, are you?" Ceelie asked, trying to conceal her laughter.

"You know what they say?"

"I'm afraid to ask," Ceelie said.

"Sometimes you gotta dance." And very discreetly, Anna did the slightest of all Snoopy Dances. "I'll be doing a better one as soon as we get back to the office," she promised.

Ceelie laughed, then pointed behind Anna.

Feeling her face already starting to flame, she turned and saw Liam standing behind her, grinning from ear to ear. "What was that?"

Before Anna could reply, Ceelie said, "That, my friend, was Anna Chapel's Snoopy Dance of Joy. Actually, it was a very watered-down version. You need to see it in full swing to get the total effect."

"Maybe I can convince her to show me later." Liam swept her into his arms and whispered in her ear, "Maybe I'll do a Dance of Joy with you."

Anna tried to picture the Liam Franklin who'd first walked into her office doing a Dance of Joy, and couldn't quite manage it. But this Liam—this man who was hugging her—she could picture dancing with joy quite handily.

"Can I talk to you a minute?" he asked.

"You two take your minute, I'll join Colm and the gang," Ceelie told them.

Anna allowed Liam to lead her to the corner of the room. "What's up?"

"A couple things. First, I don't know if I've ever really thanked you enough for everything you've done for us. And I do mean us. You helped Colm learn to spread his wings, but Anna, you've helped me as much. You've—"

"Shh. I only did my job."

"You did so much more, and you know it. But I do have one small problem."

Her stomach sank. "You're not rethinking Colm moving out, are you?"

"No, but there is a problem with it. You

see, if he moves out, I'll be stuck in that huge house all by myself. A huge house with a very nice front porch with two wicker chairs. You realize, that when Colm moves I'll have one too many wicker chairs, right?"

"Well, having too many wicker chairs would be a problem," she teased.

Serious now, he said, "I don't really want to live alone, Anna."

Before she could respond, he added, "When you were explaining your porch envy to me that first time, you said you could picture yourself coming home each night and after dinner going out to your porch and sitting in your white wicker chair. It would be nice if there was…"

"Someone sitting next to me," she whispered.

"I want to be that someone, Anna."

"Are you asking me to move in with you?"

"No. Not really. I'm asking you to marry me. I didn't plan on this now, today, but I've been thinking about it for a while. I love you, Anna. I want to live the rest of my life with you. I want Sunday mornings with coffee and the paper on the porch, with you at my side.

I want children—a family—with you. I know it's quick, but I also know it's right."

Anna wasn't sure what to say. So in the end, she simply threw herself in Liam's arms and said, "Yes," before she kissed him. Kissed the exceptional man, whom she loved more than words.

"Ew, look, they're kissing again," Colm said loudly. "They do that a lot."

"Ew," Gilly echoed.

Anna regretfully pulled back. "Should we tell them?"

"First, I have something that's just for you." Liam let her go completely and did the oddest, most endearing little butt-wiggle.

Anna burst out laughing. "What was that?"

"That, Anna, was my Liam Dance of Joy. I figure the day the woman I love agrees to marry me—" He paused. "You did agree, right?"

"Yes, I agreed."

He mock-wiped his brow. "Well, an occasion like that deserves a little Dance of Joy."

Liam pulled her close and turned to his brother and everyone else and said, "Anna's agreed to marry me."

The pandemonium continued, and Anna,

standing next to Liam, realized how lucky she was that two such very special and different men had come into her life.

She thought of Sunrise's motto about helping exceptional people lead exceptional lives.

It seemed she was surrounded by exceptional people who had given her the chance at an exceptional life. And she was going to grab it with both hands and hold on for all she was worth.

* * * * *

Rancher Ramsey Westmoreland's
temporary cook is way too attractive
for his liking.
Little does he know Chloe Burton came to
his ranch with another agenda entirely....

That man across the street had to be, without a doubt, the most handsome man she'd ever seen.

Chloe Burton's pulse beat rhythmically as he stopped to talk to another man in front of a feed store. He was tall, dark and every inch of sexy—from his Stetson to the well-worn leather boots on his feet. And from the way his jeans and Western shirt fit his broad muscular shoulders, it was quite obvious he had everything it took to separate the men from the boys. The combination was enough to corrupt any woman's mind and had her weakening even from a distance. Her body felt flushed. It was hot. Unsettled.

Over the past year the only male who had

gotten her time and attention had been the e-mail. That was simply pathetic, especially since now she was practically drooling simply at the sight of a man. Even his stance—both hands in his jeans pockets, legs braced apart, was a pose she would carry to her dreams.

And he was smiling, evidently enjoying the conversation being exchanged. He had dimples, incredibly sexy dimples in not one but both cheeks.

"What are you staring at, Clo?"

Chloe nearly jumped. She'd forgotten she had a lunch date. She glanced over the table at her best friend from college, Lucia Conyers.

"Take a look at that man across the street in the blue shirt, Lucia. Will he not be perfect for Denver's first issue of *Simply Irresistible* or what?" Chloe asked with so much excitement she almost couldn't stand it.

She was the owner of *Simply Irresistible*, a magazine for today's up-and-coming woman. Their once-a-year Irresistible Man cover, which highlighted a man the magazine felt deserved the honor, had increased sales enough for Chloe to open a Denver office.

When Lucia didn't say anything but kept staring, Chloe's smile widened. "Well?"

Lucia glanced across the booth at her. "Since you asked, I'll tell you what I see. One of the Westmorelands—Ramsey Westmoreland. And yes, he'd be perfect for the cover, but he won't do it."

Chloe raised a brow. "He'd get paid for his services, of course."

Lucia laughed and shook her head. "Getting paid won't be the issue, Clo—Ramsey is one of the wealthiest sheep ranchers in this part of Colorado. But everyone knows what a private person he is. Trust me—he won't do it."

Chloe couldn't help but smile. The man was the epitome of what she was looking for in a magazine cover and she was determined that whatever it took, he would be it.

"Umm, I don't like that look on your face, Chloe. I've seen it before and know exactly what it means."

She watched as Ramsey Westmoreland entered the store with a swagger that made her almost breathless. She *would* be seeing him again.

Look for Silhouette Desire's
HOT WESTMORELAND NIGHTS
by Brenda Jackson,
available March 9
wherever books are sold.

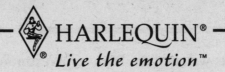

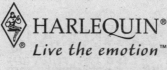

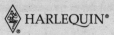

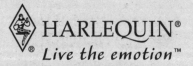

HARLEQUIN®
INTRIGUE®

BREATHTAKING ROMANTIC SUSPENSE

Shared dangers and passions lead to electrifying
romance and heart-stopping suspense!

Every month, you'll meet six new heroes
who are guaranteed to make your spine tingle
and your pulse pound. With them you'll enter
into the exciting world of Harlequin Intrigue—
where your life is on the line
and so is your heart!

THAT'S INTRIGUE—
ROMANTIC SUSPENSE
AT ITS BEST!

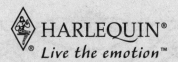

Harlequin® Historical
Historical Romantic Adventure!

Imagine a time of chivalrous
knights and unconventional ladies,
roguish rakes and impetuous
heiresses, rugged cowboys
and spirited frontierswomen—
these rich and vivid tales will
capture your imagination!

Harlequin Historical . . .
they're too good to miss!

HHDIR06

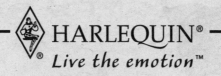

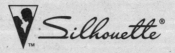